MARTA PALAZZESI

MIST

TRANSLATED BY
CHRISTOPHER TURNER

RED COMET PRESS ❧ BROOKLYN

Mist by Marta Palazzesi
This edition published in 2023 by Red Comet Press, LLC, Brooklyn, NY

English translation © 2023 Red Comet Press
Translated by Christopher Turner

Originally published in Italian as *Nebbia*
© 2019 Editrice Il Castoro Srl, Viale Andrea Doria 7 Milano
www.editriceilcastoro.it
Italian edition published by arrangement with
Grandi & Associati, Milano

Library of Congress Control Number: 2022947287
ISBN: (HB): 978-1-63655-069-5
ISBN: (Ebook): 978-1-63655-070-1
ISBN: (Audio): 978-1-63655-091-6
Cover illustration © 2023 David SanAngelo

23 24 25 26 27 TLF 10 9 8 7 6 5 4 3 2 1
Manufactured in China

RedCometPress.com

*For S and T, my inseparable
four-legged friends*

ONE

London, 1880.

For a thirteen-year-old boy, there aren't a lot of ways to get by in the slums of late-nineteenth-century London.

Obviously, the first one's thieving. But stealing from the rich is very risky. In neighborhoods like Belgravia and Kensington, with their pretty tree-lined avenues, freshly swept sidewalks, and nannies in uniforms pushing expensive baby carriages, people like us are watched by the coppers, looking for any excuse to arrest us. Stealing from the poor is even riskier: getting chased by a blood-splattered tanner or a hammer-wielding blacksmith isn't much fun.

Trust me, I know what I'm talking about.

The second way to get by in the slums is to get yourself locked up in a workhouse by the Venerable Matrons of the Most Holy Charity. But don't be fooled by their name: there's not a lot that's "most holy" or "charitable" about them.

Imagine you're standing on a bridge and looking out over the Thames. The sun's warming your skin, the sound of the water's in your ears, and your nose is being tickled by the confusion of different smells drifting up from the boats as they glide by on the river—spices from India, fruit and vegetables from the countryside, hops for the breweries, white bread for the table of some rich lord. . . . So you're standing there, in the midst of it all, enjoying your freedom in the heart of the biggest, most powerful city in the world, when a handful of women dressed in black surround you, grab you, and drag you off to a giant brick monster, where you're stripped, groomed like a horse, forced to wear a dingy uniform, and made to work ten hours a day in exchange for three lousy meals.

The way I see it, you might even start to miss the blood-splattered tanner.

The last way to survive in the slums of late-nineteenth-century London is the noble art of getting by on your wits. That's how I do it.

"Hey, Nucky, why don't you tell us about the Great Stink of '58?"

It was a warm morning in late June. My friends and I had been working on the muddy banks of the Thames since dawn. We'd already collected a good amount of stuff: a few copper nails, a wooden pipe, a leather boot. When we sold them, we'd have enough money to eat for a couple of days.

I straightened up, yawned, stretched, and looked around. The gray water of the Thames sparkled in the sunlight, and, on the opposite bank, the dome of St. Paul's Cathedral stood out white against the blue sky like a mountain of sugar.

"Well?" I asked.

Nucky gave me a half smile without stopping picking through the mud. The Great Stink of 1858 was his favorite story, and, even though we knew it by heart, Nucky always added some extra gruesome detail or some spicy new anecdote. Not everyone shared his enthusiasm for the story, though.

"Oh, Clay, no. Not *again*," Tod muttered, kneeling beside me, up to his elbows in mud.

"What are you saying?" Nucky snapped.

"That I'm sick of listening to you jabbering on about dead bodies, dung, and animal innards," Tod answered. "We get it: in 1858 the Thames stank of dead animals. What a great story."

"In the summer of 1858, the Thames did not just stink of 'dead animals'!" Nucky said angrily, as if keeping the memory of the Great Stink alive was somehow his responsibility. I never understood why he was so fixated by it. When I first met him, he was already obsessed.

Nucky cleared his throat and punched the sky, ready to launch into one of his detailed accounts. "It hadn't rained for weeks, and the river had dropped by yards and yards. Queen Victoria and Prince Albert took a boat trip but had to go back to the palace because the stink was so bad. The Thames had turned into a putrid, pus-filled pool of entrails, excrement, maggoty corpses—"

"Weren't they flies?" I asked. "Yesterday you said the corpses were covered in flies."

"What difference does it make?" Nucky snapped, wiping his nose on the bottom of his shirt. "Before they're flies, they're maggots."

"Damn, Nucky, you're obsessed," Tod said in disgust. "And you," he said, turning to me, "stop encouraging him or, sooner or later, I'll have to shut him up once and for—"

Whack!

A ball of mud glanced off Tod's head and slapped into the muck behind him. Purple in the face, Tod stood up and pointed his finger at Nucky, who was trying hard not to laugh.

"I'm going to give you a damn good beat—"

"Tod!"

"What, Clay?! You can't always stick up for him just because he's little!"

I shook my head and pointed to some dark shapes that were slipping and sliding toward us like a silent swarm of beetles.

Tod followed my gaze and forgot about teaching Nucky a lesson. "The dogs. They still don't know that this is our part of the bank?"

"It doesn't look like it," I sighed.

I didn't feel like fighting that morning. Being a mud lark was hard enough without having to keep on fighting off other gangs.

Everyone knew Nucky, Tod, and me as the Terrors of Blackfriars Bridge, and it hadn't been easy conquering that bank of the Thames. It was ours now, though, and there was no way we were going to share it with other mud larks. Everyone knew that the best places were the ones closest to the bridges, since it wasn't that unusual for people to throw a few coins or food scraps from a passing carriage. And that was exactly how the three of us had grabbed this spot years ago: by fighting with another gang of mud larks for a half crown thrown by some rich lord who'd watched us fight as he smoked his pipe with a grin on his face from up on the bridge.

"Come on, lads!" he'd shouted. "Put on a good show for me!"

And we did put on a good show. Fighting like angry terriers, Tod, Nucky, and I had made the other mud larks turn tail and run, even though there were more of them and they were bigger than us.

"I'm too old for this," I said, shaking my head, as Nucky and Tod came alongside me, ready for battle.

I let Tod do the talking. He was the biggest of us, and, with his messy black hair, dark eyes, thick eyebrows, and scarred face, he was pretty good at scaring his enemies. Getting on the wrong side of Tod wasn't a good idea. *Think before you act* and *stay calm* just weren't in his vocabulary.

Nucky, on the other hand, was blond, pale, and looked puny and sickly. He made up for it, though, by being cunning. He was the one who negotiated with the people who bought the things we pulled out of the mud of the riverbank, and he always got the best prices.

Then there was me, not too big and not too small, with brown hair and eyes, and an anonymous enough face so that people didn't notice me. I always seemed to be calm, and that made my enemies underestimate me, which was often an advantage.

There were six mud larks invading our territory. Once we got a closer look at them, though, they didn't look like they'd come to fight. They were smaller than us and had the confused look of someone who still hasn't worked out their place in the world. For a moment, they reminded me of myself when I was five—when, after being orphaned, I'd ended up without a place to live or a grown-up to turn to. I'd wandered the banks of the river for a few days, eating scraps of food I found out the back of pubs and taverns, knowing that I wasn't going to last very long like that. Then, out of nowhere, Old Sal had appeared with his long beard and hooked staff. He'd taken me under his wing and taught me about life as a mud lark.

The Terrors of Blackfriars Bridge had their territory and reputation to defend. So even though I felt sorry for these brats (*compassion* was another word Tod didn't know, while Nucky only ever thought about the Great Stink of '58), we couldn't be too kind to them.

"This is our territory," Tod said, getting straight to the point. "Clear off."

The leader of the other mud larks, a skinny, redheaded kid, put his hands up to signal peace. "We don't want any trouble. We just want to pass through."

"To go where?" I asked.

"Vauxhall Bridge," he answered.

"Bad idea. It's taken." I looked at Tod for confirmation. "By the Blonde and her Scabby Dogs, right?"

Tod nodded and touched the scar under his right ear, a souvenir the Blonde had given him after a little misunderstanding a couple of years ago. It was a miracle that we'd gotten away alive, to be honest. But that's another story.

"They're not people you want to play games with," I warned. "If I were you, I'd keep well clear of them."

The children exchanged worried glances. "Do you have anything to eat?" the redheaded one asked hopefully.

"Of course, and would you like a nice cup of tea to go with it?" Nucky grinned.

"Of course we don't," growled Tod. "And we don't have any time to waste, either. Clear off, brat."

"I can pay," he said quickly. "Well, not exactly," he admitted to Nucky's skeptical glare. He reached into his jacket pocket and rummaged about for a moment. "Here," he said, pulling out a small wooden box. "I found it this morning on the Isle of Dogs." He held it out to me, and, after a quick glance at Nucky and Tod, I took it.

It was about the size of my hand and, under the layer of dry mud, you could make out quality inlay work. I rubbed it against my trousers to clean it and then opened it, sliding the wooden lid back along its groove. Inside was a deck of hand-painted tarot cards in perfect condition.

Nucky came over to get a better look. "Crikey," he said, "that's quality stuff. Look at those colors."

I closed the box and threw it back to the redhead, who caught it. "Sell them. You'll get enough money for bread and cheese."

He shook his head. "I don't know who to sell them to."

"This isn't a job for lazy brats," Tod growled. The conversation had gone on too long for his liking. "You have to work hard if you want to get by. Now clear off or I'll throttle the lot of you!"

The redheaded boy and his gang set off again, parading past us with their heads bowed and a gloomy air.

"Mad," Tod said, rolling up his sleeves and getting back to digging in the mud.

"Aye," Nucky agreed.

"Giving food to a bunch of lazy . . . What did they take us for?!"

"Aye," Nucky agreed again.

"As if we didn't have enough problems already. Right, Clay? . . . *Clay?*"

"Umm, aye," I muttered distractedly as I watched the mud larks walking away.

"Oh, here we go again!" Tod groaned. "You're going to do it, aren't you?"

I answered him with a grin. Then I shouted after the redhead, "Hey, you! Come back!"

"Damn, Clay," sighed Tod. "You're too soft."

"Those cards are worth a lot, and he's too stupid to know it," I answered.

Tod rattled off half a dozen bad words of the worst kind, while Nucky did his best not to laugh. "Clay's right," he said. "Those cards are wasted on him."

"Aye, to be sure," Tod grumbled. "Why don't you take Clay's side for a change."

I left Nucky and Tod alone for their umpteenth argument and went over to the mud larks. "Here." I took some bread wrapped in cloth out of my jacket pocket and handed it to the red-haired boy. "It's a loaf of bread. It's fresh."

It really was. Old Sal had given it to me that morning when I'd called in on him at his shack. He'd come by it through strange circumstances from a maid in Kensington, his latest romantic interest. Like always, I hadn't wanted to know too much about it.

"Those tarot cards are worth a lot more, though," I said.

The redhead didn't seem to have a lot of business sense. Without thinking, he threw the wooden box at me and grabbed the bread with a hungry look in his eyes. Then, after shoving the loaf down the front of his shirt, he ran off, followed by his unfortunate associates.

"I'm going to the Queen's Tavern," I told Tod and Nucky, waving the tarot cards in the air. "Maybe Madame Lorna will have some customers interested in these."

"A spoon!" cried Nucky, pulling a piece of silverware out of the mud. He cleaned it on his shirt and then gave it a good bite. "Pewter," he said expertly. "Worse than silver, better than wood." He put the spoon in his pocket and looked at me. "Good idea, Clay. Madame Lorna will know who to sell them to."

"That is if they make it to Lorna," Tod grumbled. "Knowing Clay, he'll give them to the first bowlegged fortune teller he meets."

"Thanks for the vote of confidence." I laughed. "I'll be back later."

Before going up onto the wharf, I walked a few dozen yards to find a slightly less filthy part of the river to wash the mud off myself. Not that there was any chance that Queen Victoria would set foot in the pub named after her, but if there was one thing that Madame Lorna wouldn't put up with in her place, it was muddy mud larks and toshers, underground scavengers, who stank of sewage.

Speaking of toshers, there were a couple of them cleaning up right where I stopped. "Hello," I said as I started to undress.

"Hello," they answered back. They were a little older than me, around sixteen or seventeen, and had the typical unhealthy look of people who spent most of the day digging around under the ground. Even though London's sewers were full of better stuff than what you found along the river, I much preferred working outside. The dark, the stink, the suffocating brick walls . . . The way I saw it, a life in a cage wasn't worth living.

I picked up a stone and scrubbed my arms and legs with it, before looking after my face and hair. When I was fairly well polished—as polished as a mud lark can be—I washed my clothes. Then, still wet from head to toe, I dressed and set off toward Cheapside, the area behind St. Paul's Cathedral, a maze of narrow, winding streets lined with the shops of craftsmen and merchants.

I walked along Bread Street, trying not to drool too much over the brown-crusted loaves in the shop windows, to where it met Cheapside. There, on the corner between the wide, busy street full of horse-drawn carriages and trams and the narrow Milk Lane, was the Queen's Tavern, run by Madame Lorna. It was a typical pub, with black wood paneling, big rectangular windows made up of little glass squares, and a sign painted with gold letters lit by lanterns.

Even though it was early, the place was already full. Besides the usual crowd of idlers, some workers were taking a break, creating a weird mixture of shapes and colors: bakers, their hair white with flour, stood alongside knife sharpeners with faces black from grinding, stocky potato sellers with dirty nails, and flower girls with baskets full of colors.

I pushed my way through the crowd to the bar. Madame Lorna was there. She was a big woman who must have weighed two hundred pounds, with red cheeks, coal-black hair, and a spotless apron over her huge belly. She was busy doing one of her favorite things (after drinking and eating), namely, harassing her husband, a little man with a low forehead who probably didn't weigh much more than ninety pounds—shoes, hat, and walking stick included.

"Alfie, I've told you a thousand times that you have to watch out for those rats!" Madame Lorna thundered, slapping her hand on the counter. "I hope you're not expecting me to go down into the cellar!"

The poor man's head drooped between his shoulders. "No, no, of course not, dear."

"No, what?"

"You don't have to go down to the cellar."

"So how are you going to fix the problem?"

"Ch-cheese?"

"Cheese?!" Madame Lorna thundered. "You think I should waste my good cheese on stinking rats?"

"No, no, of course not!"

"How about a cat, Alfie?"

"Y-you want to feed the rats a c-cat? I g-guess that might work. . . ."

"Yes, maybe with some mashed potatoes," Madame Lorna retorted in exasperation. "For heaven's sake, Alfie, go out and find a damned cat and put it in the cellar. Alive!"

Poor Alfie was just waiting for a chance to escape from his wife's clutches. He stammered something indistinct and slipped away from the bar, rushing toward the door with all the enthusiasm of a castaway a few strokes from shore.

"Oh, Clay," Madame Lorna said offhandedly. "I didn't see you there."

Liar. She'd known full well I was there. That's why she'd raged at her husband like that: she loved an audience.

Madame Lorna poured herself a small glass of Pimm's and swallowed it in a gulp. She offered me some, but I shook my head. "Do you know how much money that bastard James Pimm made with this concoction?" she asked. "My mother knew him. He was a nobody who started out selling oysters on the street right behind this pub. Then he came up with this stuff," she said, holding up the bottle of amber liquid and then slamming it violently down on the counter, "and it made him rich!"

"It must be good, then," I said after Madame Lorna had poured herself a second glass.

She frowned at me and drained that glass, too. "Where have you left your delinquent associates?"

"They're working," I answered, sitting on a stool. I took the box of tarot cards out of my still-wet jacket pocket. "I want to sell these. Would any of your customers be interested?"

Obviously, I didn't mean her regulars at the pub but the group of emptyheaded ladies whom Madame Lorna gave "séance lessons" once a week. A gust of wind, a swish of a curtain, a candle going out, and they began to howl as if they were possessed, convinced that their dearly departed were trying to communicate with them.

As Old Sal always said, "Top hat and cane, rich and no brain." And based on Madame Lorna's stories, he was probably right. The richer you are, the dumber you are.

The woman opened the wooden box and carefully examined its contents. "Quality stuff," she said. "But my clients are too respectable to have anything like this in their homes. Their husbands would get suspicious."

"What an idiot," I muttered to myself. "I didn't think about that. You always meet in secret, don't you?"

Madame Lorna nodded. "It would be an utter scandal if people found out that Duchess Whatsit and the Countess of Thingamabob visit a woman like me."

I got up from the stool and put the tarot cards back in my pocket. "I'll try around Whitechapel. Maybe I'll . . ."

Taa-daa! Taa-daa! Boom! Boom! Boom!

"What's that racket?" cried Madame Lorna, looking out at the street.

Just then, the door swung open and a boy ran in and stopped in the middle of the pub, his face red and sweaty. "A circus parade!" he cried. "There are camels! Elephants! Clowns! And . . . and . . ." Choked by excitement, the boy gasped for air for a few seconds as he looked for words that would do justice to the event. But he soon gave up and bolted back out into the street.

A few moments later, I was walking along Cheapside with most of the neighborhood, waiting for the parade. It was pretty common to see spectacular parades announcing the arrival of a circus in the city. They'd be led by a brightly colored wagon followed by lots of animals and performers. This circus was no exception.

The first thing I saw was a huge red and gold wagon pulled

by six white horses with plumes on their heads. The wheels were as tall as me, with swirls and arabesques between the spokes. The sides were covered with spectacular carved lions with their mouths wide open and elephants with their trunks in the air.

"Bless me!" someone behind me said. "What a spectacle!"

"They're from up north," someone else explained. "They've taken their show everywhere, but it's the first time they've come to London."

When the wagon was close enough, I read the words carved on the side: "Smith & Sparrow's Amazing Circus— Since 1789."

"Look! The elephants!" a child cried out.

"Damn . . . ," I whispered. I'd seen quite a few parades, but I'd never seen such big elephants. They must have been at least eighteen feet tall, with leathery gray skin, long swinging trunks, and fancy scarlet harnesses. On the back of each elephant—I counted twelve of them—a juggler in costume was balancing a ball on his nose.

After the elephants came the camels, angry-looking beasts with humped backs. They vaguely reminded me of the pompous City bankers with their bushy beards and heavy eyelids.

"What's that?" a woman next to me asked.

The last thing in the spectacular parade was a second wagon, just as big as the first but painted blue and silver. It was carrying a giant cage with dark bars, inside of which a man in a long, glittering cloak was making frightening noises as he threw handbills to the crowd.

I grabbed one of the colorful pieces of paper.

"What does it say? What does it say?" a child with a soot-stained face urged, pulling at my sleeve. "I can't read!"

"It says they've got a wolf in the circus," I answered. "The last living wolf in the United Kingdom of Great Britain and Ireland."

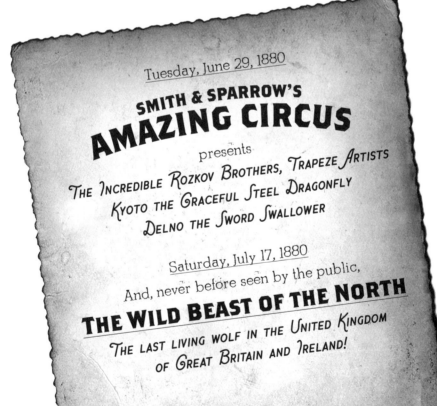

Tuesday, June 29, 1880

**SMITH & SPARROW'S
AMAZING CIRCUS**

presents

THE INCREDIBLE ROZKOV BROTHERS, TRAPEZE ARTISTS
KYOTO THE GRACEFUL STEEL DRAGONFLY
DELNO THE SWORD SWALLOWER

Saturday, July 17, 1880

And, never before seen by the public,

THE WILD BEAST OF THE NORTH

THE LAST LIVING WOLF IN THE UNITED KINGDOM
OF GREAT BRITAIN AND IRELAND!

"Imagine that!" exclaimed a nearby potato seller. "There haven't been any wolves for three hundred years!"

"It's just a trick to take our money," commented a knife grinder. "Mark my words, it'll be nothing but a fat dog."

"A wolf?" The child stared at me with his mouth open. "It really says that?"

I nodded. "Aye."

"And do you believe it?" he asked.

Before I could answer, I was attracted to a person riding a mule just behind the blue and silver wagon. She was a thin old woman, dressed from head to toe in red, with lots of gold rings in her ears and around her wrists. Beside her, a dark-haired girl who looked about thirteen in a flouncy gold dress was dancing to a tambourine.

"A didicoy,*" muttered the potato seller, crossing herself. "Don't look into her face or she'll give you the evil eye!"

"Don't talk nonsense," snapped the knife grinder. "It's just some old woman wearing a whole lot of junk."

As the parade disappeared around St. Paul's, I thought to myself that the man was probably right. She probably wasn't a real didicoy, just a woman dressed up like a traveler. But I didn't care either way. As far as I was concerned, I'd just found a buyer for the tarot cards.

---

* A traveler of part Romani descent.

Besides the chance of doing a good deal, I admit that my decision to go to the circus was also out of curiosity. The only wolves I'd ever seen were in pictures hanging in the windows of printing houses. The idea of seeing one live fascinated me.

"The last living wolf in the United Kingdom of Great Britain and Ireland," I muttered to myself, looking at the colorful handbill again. "Who knows . . ."

There was only one way to find out.

TWO

Smith & Sparrow's Amazing Circus had set up its gigantic scarlet tent in a large clearing surrounded by a wooden fence near Westminster Bridge. Colorful wagons were standing around the tent in a circle, and I was amazed by the number of people swarming around the area. Besides the performers, who were easy to recognize in their makeup and costumes, there were dozens of lads and workers carrying tools, pushing wheelbarrows, and dragging sacks. I immediately noticed (and I confess that I stood looking at her for a good five minutes with my mouth gaping) a beautiful woman with translucent skin, almond-shaped eyes, and shiny black hair tied in a bun. She was walking on a rope stretched between two wagons. She must be the

Steel Dragonfly that the handbill talked about, I thought, as I started walking again without taking my eyes off her.

A little farther on, I was stopped in my tracks again (for a very different reason) by the sight of a man in a singlet with oily, bulging muscles and a thick dark beard, as he stuck a sword about a foot long down his throat. Delno, the sword swallower.

Hurry up, Clay, I told myself, before climbing over the fence. It's not going to be easy finding the didicoy here.

And I wasn't wrong. After about half an hour, I'd come up with nothing but four shoves from some unfriendly workers, a suspicious brown lump stuck to the sole of my boot, and a nasty glare from a man, probably a watchman, on a horse.

But no sign of the didicoy.

Much less of the wolf.

I found a place behind a stack of crates and pulled the box of tarot cards out from my jacket pocket, glancing over at the scarlet tent. The entrances were guarded by beefy men with beards—they obviously wanted to scare away nosy people like me. Without some incredible stroke of luck, I'd never be able to sneak inside.

But that stroke of luck came in the form of a painful blow to my chest.

"*Oww!*"

"Oww's right! What are you doing hanging around back here?"

Rubbing my chest, I looked at the girl who'd just jumped me. I recognized her immediately: she was the girl I'd seen with the didicoy in the parade.

"Well?" she asked, staring at me with piercing blue eyes. "What's wrong with you? Cat got your tongue?"

"I'm sorry," I answered. "I was looking for . . ."

"A way to sneak into the big top?" she suggested. "You're already the fifth one to try today. And, I warn you, things didn't go too well for the other four."

"No, no. I'm not here to sneak into the tent." I showed her the box of tarot cards. "I want to sell these. I saw the parade in Cheapside today and thought the didicoy might be interested."

"The didicoy's my grandmother," she replied. "And she's got lots of tarot cards already." My disappointment must have been obvious, since, after sighing, she said, "I can let you show them to her. An extra deck always comes in handy."

"Thank you . . ."

"I'm Olivia, but everyone calls me Ollie."

"I'm Clay."

"Clay? Good name for a mud lark."

"How do you know I'm a mud lark?"

"You've got dry mud behind your ears and under your nails."

Feeling embarrassed, I tried to take her attention off my grimy appearance. "So can we go see your grandmother?"

"She's busy at the moment. Give me the cards and I'll show them to her as soon as she's free. If she's interested, I'll pay you tomorrow. If she's not, I'll give them back."

I thought about what Tod would say if I went back to him and Nucky empty-handed, and giggled.

"What's so funny?" asked Ollie.

"Nothing, nothing. It's just that my associates won't like it." I gave her the box anyway. "Half a crown."

"A bit expensive."

"Quality costs money," I answered, trying to show some of Nucky's confidence in negotiations.

"I'll see what I can do." Ollie slipped the tarot cards into a pocket of her red and gold dress, and, for a moment, I had the horrible feeling that I'd just been cheated.

"Well, see you tomorrow morning," said Ollie. "Be here around eleven."

"Wait!" I stopped her.

"So you really did want to sneak into the big top?" She grinned.

"No," I answered. "I mean, well, I'm not saying I wouldn't like a look inside. I was wondering . . . ," I lowered my voice, "do you really have a wolf like it says on the handbills?"

A shadow passed over Ollie's blue eyes. "Yes, he's in the menagerie with the other animals."

"Would it be too much to ask you for a look?"

Ollie thought for a moment. "It will cost you."

Nucky would have liked her. "How much?"

"The tarot cards for a florin."

On second thoughts, he wouldn't have liked her at all.

"All right," I answered, holding out my hand.

Ollie shook it. "I thought you mud larks were smarter than that."

"So did I."

"Come with me. The menagerie's just past the big top."

I followed Ollie around the field, trying to be just as quick as her at dodging, jumping, and avoiding obstacles and people, but the place was like a huge maze full of traps.

"Look out!" Ollie yelled before a flaming dagger shot past my face. "What are you doing there? You're right in the middle of where our knife thrower practices!"

I looked around bewildered. It didn't seem to me that I was right in the middle of anything, but when a second fiery dagger almost scalped me before digging into a board behind me, I hurried to catch up with Ollie and didn't leave her side again.

After passing the tent and a row of colorful wagons, we

came out into a scrubby clearing in the middle of which was a second tent, much smaller than the first and whitish in color. It was also surrounded by wagons. But unlike the others I'd seen, their sides were iron bars. Inside them, animals were either sleeping or eating.

"They keep the more harmless ones out here," Ollie explained as we walked toward the tent. "Monkeys, birds, dogs."

I looked at the animals locked in the wagons, but as soon as my eyes met with a pair of monkey's, I turned away, feeling a knot in my stomach. I'd never liked animals much. Actually, the seagulls that my associates and I often had to fight along the river for an apple core or a piece of bread had come very close to being beaten with a stone or a stick quite a few times. But . . . at least that was a fair fight. We had stones; the seagulls had wings. This, though, didn't seem to be fair.

"What's wrong? Are you scared of monkeys?" Ollie asked when she saw me turn away.

"No," I answered. "It's just that . . ."

"What?"

I shrugged. "Nothing. So where's the wolf?"

"Be patient," answered Ollie, walking around the outside of the tent. Roars, barking, and eerie hissing noises were coming from inside. When we got to the other side, I saw the elephants from the parade about twenty yards from us. They were tied to huge logs buried in the ground and were flicking their tails to shoo away insects.

"Don't they get hot standing there in the sun?" I asked.

"Are you joking? Those things come from Africa. It's hot enough to kill you over there. Now shut up, we mustn't get caught."

Ollie stopped about twenty paces farther on, near a long tear in the side of the tent. Someone had made a halfhearted effort to patch it up, so that all Ollie needed to do was give it a tug and it came open.

"Guests first," she announced grandly. "Hide behind the crates."

A little hesitantly, I bent down and slipped through the opening. The second I was inside the tent, I was hit by the smell of the place and the noises made by the animals. I crouched down among some crates that were just in front of the tear as Ollie had told me to do, then craned my neck to get a better look.

Arranged in a circle around the ring in the middle, there were numerous cages with the animals divided up by species inside them. Right ahead of me were three big lions, two males with huge manes and a smaller female. Beside them, but some distance away, an enormous cat with black fur and yellow eyes paced nervously back and forth in its cramped cage.

I pointed to it. "What's that?"

"A panther," said Ollie, who'd just crouched down beside me. "You've never seen one before?"

"No."

"Smith and Sparrow bought it from another circus last month."

I continued looking at the different cages. I saw a big brown bear with a white collar around its neck, a couple of tigers, and four spotted pigs.

"The wolf's in that one," said Ollie, pointing to a smallish cage covered by a black tarpaulin. The cage was the farthest one from the entrance and a good distance from the other animals. "Come on, let me show you. . . ."

"Let's see if that bastard will cooperate today!"

Ollie grabbed me by the arm and motioned to me to keep quiet. A moment later, a man and a boy stepped into the tent. With his narrow, pointy nose and tiny eyes, the man immediately made me think of a bird of prey. Even his hair, which was fair, fine, and thinning, looked like a bird's ruffled feathers. Although he was very skinny, his forearms were wiry with muscle. In one hand he was holding a whip. The boy was much bigger. I thought he looked like Tod, with dark hair and eyes, muscular arms, and a face covered in scars. Unlike Tod, though, this boy had evil in his eyes.

And I knew evil very well: I'd seen it many times in the mud larks along the river. "There's a fine line between survival instinct and evil, Clay," Old Sal had told me on my eighth birthday. "We mud larks have to fight to keep control of our territory, but that doesn't give us the right to mistreat people weaker than us. In other words, only ever fight those who can fight back," he'd said, handing me a small knife with a decorated handle. He'd made it himself, fitting an old blade into a piece of exotic wood that must have gone missing off some ship back from India or Africa. I still had it, hidden in a pocket inside my jacket. I'd never used it and hoped I'd never have to.

This boy, though, looked like someone who'd have used it without a second thought and might have even enjoyed it.

"Parson, the tamer," Ollie whispered, pointing to the man. "And that's his son, Hiram."

As they walked by the cages, many of the animals backed away. Hiram laughed and took out the truncheon he had tucked into his trousers. When he got to the bear's cage, he smashed it violently against the iron bars. The animal, one of the few that hadn't paid any attention to them, howled with pain and tried to hide at the back of the cage.

"So you remember this, hey?" Hiram grinned, waving the truncheon in the air.

"Hiram," his father said, "stop wasting time and get the noose."

"Noose?" I started.

"Shh," Ollie silenced me.

Hiram disappeared for a moment behind the lions' cage. When he came back out, he had a long pole with a noose on the end in one hand and a stick with an iron spike in the other.

"Ready, son?" asked Parson.

"Can't wait to have some fun!" Hiram answered with a grin.

His father gave him a dark glare. "This isn't fun. It's work."

Hiram lost some of his cockiness. "Aye, Father."

Parson stood in front of the wolf's cage. "So, you devil, are you in a good mood today?" he asked. Then, with a snap, he pulled off the tarpaulin.

And that was the first time I saw Mist.

"Beautiful, isn't he?" Ollie whispered.

No, the wolf wasn't just beautiful. The wolf was windswept moors, races through forests, nights spent sniffing out prey, howling at the moon. . . . And there it all was, right in front of me. Locked in a cage.

"What's wrong with you?" Ollie touched my shoulder. "Are you disappointed?"

Disappointed by this creature with his silver coat and huge amber eyes? He was the most amazing thing I'd ever seen. And I knew straightaway that he was the most amazing thing I'd see in my life.

"No, but . . ."

"But?"

Just then, the wolf let out a furious howl and bared his teeth. His ears and the fur on his neck stood straight up. Parson and Hiram weren't impressed. In fact, the animal trainer burst out laughing, walked over to the cage, and unlocked it with a click. "Come here, Hiram. Be ready."

The boy went over to his father, firmly gripping the pole with the noose. As soon as the man had opened the cage door a few inches, Hiram slipped the pole inside and tried to put the rope around the wolf's neck. He missed by a mile, and I smiled.

But when Hiram stuck the pole with the iron spike between the bars, my smile vanished.

"Come on, son, get it round its neck!" urged his father.

If only the wolf hurled himself against the door, I thought. Parson wouldn't be able to hold it back, and then . . .

Hiram brought the noose closer to the wolf's neck, while he stuck the spike into his side. "Take that, you devil!" he cried with a grin as the animal howled with pain.

"No!" I screamed.

"Stop!" Ollie grabbed me by the arm. "Get back down!"

It was hard, but I crouched back down behind the crates. Parson and Hiram had been too busy with the wolf to notice anything.

"They can't do that!" I protested.

"Of course they can," Ollie said. "We're a circus. How do you think we train the animals?"

"I don't know. Not like that."

"It's the only way. Parson and Hiram are all that separates them from us. Without them, they'd kill us."

I couldn't believe it. Was Ollie defending Parson and Hiram?

"Well, maybe that's exactly what you all deserve!"

And, without waiting for an answer, I ducked out through the tear in the canvas and ran back to the river.

THREE

"I remember these Spanish tiles. You almost croaked bringing them up from the bottom of the river."

Old Sal gave me a probing look. "Did you come here to talk about my floor?"

I stopped pacing around Old Sal's shack and sank down into one of the armchairs in front of the cold fireplace. It was almost midnight. I hadn't been able to sleep, so, half an hour ago, I'd left the riverside shack I shared with Nucky and Tod to go for a walk. Like always, I'd eventually found myself going in the direction of Old Sal's home, certain he'd be awake. And I wasn't wrong. Once I was past the fisherman's wharf, I'd seen him waiting for me at the door, with his pipe in his mouth like always, his felt hat on his head, and his perfectly (and inexplicably) manicured silver beard. I had no idea how old Sal was, but he'd looked exactly the same for as long as I'd known him.

"What's the matter, lad? Problems with your associates?"

"Tod and Nucky? No. I mean, sooner or later Tod's going to break Nucky's head, but work's fine."

"So is it a girl?"

I shook my head. "If only."

Old Sal took a long drag on his silver pipe. "Wait a few years, and we'll talk about it."

"Aye," I murmured, unconvinced. To tell the truth, we mud larks weren't exactly in demand for romance, so I doubted we'd ever really talk about the subject that much.

"So, if it's not about work or love, what's bothering you?"

I sprang up from my chair and started pacing again on the Spanish tiles. Old Sal's place was the only mud lark home I knew of with a floor worthy of the name. After all, Old Sal was also the only mud lark who smoked a silver pipe, had a full set of buttons on his shirts and trousers, and lived in a house full of things that you'd usually only find in the houses of the rich, like a Flemish harpsichord with boxwood keys, a collection of Chinese porcelain vases, and an ornate seventeenth-century lectern that Old Sal used to hang up his coat.

"It's hard to explain," I answered, because it really was. The image of the caged wolf continued to haunt me. But why? In my short life, I'd seen far worse things than that. Children dying of hunger. Parents who, to support their other children, would sell off the oldest one to some shipping company as a cabin or scullery boy. Why was I so upset about an animal? An animal that, if he had the opportunity, wouldn't hesitate to tear me to pieces.

"Try," said Old Sal.

I sat back down in the armchair. "I saw an injustice today," I tried. After all, that's what it was. "But the thing is . . . I see injustices every day. And I never do anything because that's how things work here. But . . ."

"But?"

"But this time I feel like I have to do something."

"So follow your instincts."

"If you knew what I'm talking about, you wouldn't say that. You'd tell me to forget it and think about important things."

"And what would they be?"

"Digging. Getting the best price. Defending our territory."

Old Sal was silent for a long while, staring at the nonexistent flames in the fireplace. "I must be a very bad teacher if I was the one who made you believe those things are important," he eventually said.

"But . . ."

Old Sal silenced me with a raised hand. His pale eyes danced around the room. "In a few years, none of this will be left. My possessions will end up being sold, and people will haggle over the prices. They'll end up decorating some house, and no one will know who they belonged to or what kind of person he was. You see, lad, no matter how much money I make, no matter how many beautiful vases or clothes or pieces of furniture I collect in my life, there'll come a time when none of it will matter. If anything of me survives in this world, it will be the memories of the people whose paths crossed with mine."

Old Sal took a long drag on his pipe. For a moment, his face disappeared behind a thick wall of smoke. "The world's full of injustices, Clay," he started again. "Too many to think of changing it. But no battle is more important than any other battle. What really matters is the battle you choose to fight. However small, insignificant, or pointless it might seem compared to all the disgusting things in the world, in the end it will be all that remains of you." Old Sal got up from his chair and walked to the door.

"What if I lose?" I asked. "Sal, what if I lose this battle? What if it turns out to be just a waste of time?"

"The way I see it, Clay, the lower the chances of an

undertaking succeeding, the greater the value of the person who dedicates himself to it."

That said, Old Sal walked toward the river and was soon lost among the reflections off the water.

"Hey, look who it is! One of the Blackfriars brats!"

I looked up and found myself staring at Vauxhall Bridge and its great arches of dark stone. The Blonde's gang was standing on the riverbank and looked ready for a fight. Without realizing it, I'd trespassed into their territory, and trespassing into the Scabby Dogs' territory was no better idea than trying to cheat them. My associates and I knew that all too well.

A couple of years ago, Nucky had traded some pewter teapots with one of them, passing them off as silver. In exchange, he'd been given two real silver brooches, which he sold at the Whitechapel Market in under half an hour. We'd used the money to buy bread, cheese, honey, and even a few half-good apples. When the Scabby Dog had realized he'd been tricked, a fight had broken out, and Tod, who was defending Nucky, almost had an ear cut clean off. He only hadn't been killed because the coppers had arrived in time, attracted by the furious screaming from the riverbank.

Since then, relations between the Terrors of Blackfriars Bridge and the Scabby Dogs had been a little tense.

The Blonde stepped forward with her hands on her hips, her stubby legs planted on the ground, and her chin high. She was bigger than I remembered, with straw-colored hair halfway down her back, an almost lipless mouth, and big blue bulbous fish eyes. She was in every way a creature of the river, but she was as good with her fists as any of the laborers who crowded the docks.

"What are you doing here, Clay?" she asked.

I lifted my hands. "I'm not looking for trouble."

"Too late for that," one of the Scabby Dogs said, grinning.

"Shut up," the Blonde growled. She looked me up and down as carefully as if she were working out a price for something. "Have you heard about the raid, too?"

"A raid? No, but I wouldn't worry," I answered. "Old Sal always manages to get on the right side of the coppers."

"This time it's not the coppers," the Blonde answered.

"Who is it, then? Those mad women from the workhouse?"

"No."

"Who, then?"

The Blonde raised her eyebrows. "Men from the factory."

I immediately understood. This was a big problem. You could bribe the police and outrun the Venerable Matrons of the Most Holy Charity, but the men from the factories were another thing completely. They worked at night, entering the shacks along the river armed with ropes and sticks. In no time, you'd be bound, gagged, and tossed into the back of a cart, headed for one of the many cloth factories on the outskirts of the city. And once you were chained up to a loom inside one of them, there was no escape.

"Sleep with one eye open," said the Blonde. "Now clear off."

"What?!" protested a Scabby Dog. "You're letting him go just like that? He's trespassing on our territory. We've got to teach him a lesson!"

The Blonde silenced the girl with a ferocious glare, and I took my opportunity to get away fast, after thanking her for the unexpected kindness. Not only had she saved me from a beating, she'd warned me about the raids.

I absolutely have to talk to Tod and Nucky, I thought nervously. Tod and I are starting to get too big for the looms, but Nucky, with his skinny fingers, is the sort of worker they look for.

I turned on my heel and walked back down the river toward Blackfriars Bridge. The day promised to be hot, and a sickly sweet smell came off the Thames. The older mud larks had said that it would rain next week, and the river, after rising and retreating, would leave a lot of treasure on its muddy banks. As disgusting as it might sound, the highest-prized treasures were the corpses of rich people, who, after a glass too many, ended up doing something stupid, like walking on the railing of a bridge and falling into the water with all their precious watches and jewels on.

I reached my destination when the bells of St. Paul's were striking twelve. I felt a gnawing feeling in my stomach: I'd missed my appointment with Ollie. Something had stopped me from going to the circus that morning.

Maybe I'm not as brave as I think I am, I told myself. Maybe, despite all those fine words with Old Sal, I really don't have the guts to do what—

"Listen, darling, you'd better get out of here. We've got no time to waste on you!"

Nucky's hysterical voice interrupted my thoughts. I lifted my head and found myself looking at a scene that was unusual to say the least. Ollie, dressed in her colorful clothes and with her black hair tied back in a long braid, was staring in amazement at Nucky, who was red in the face and waving a bony fist under her nose.

"All I said was that you did a bad deal," Ollie said with a shrug. "You should have gotten a lot more for those spoons."

"I know how much they were worth!" Nucky barked threateningly.

Meanwhile, Tod was looking on, giggling with his arms folded. "Your friend's got a lot of pluck," he said when I joined him.

"She's not my friend," I answered, almost without thinking.

Ollie gave me a resentful look. "Don't worry, I'm not keen to be your life companion, either." She pulled something out of her dress pocket and threw it at me. Tod, who had better reflexes than mine, grabbed the tarot box before it hit me in the nose.

"Didn't you say you sold them?" Nucky snapped.

"Yes, well, almost," I stammered.

"Actually, he left them with me without wanting a penny in return," Ollie snorted.

If possible, Nucky's face turned even redder. "What?!"

"Come on, Nucky, keep calm," said Tod. "At least she brought them back."

"Exactly," said Ollie. She pointed a finger at me and, for a moment, I was afraid she was going to give me the evil eye. "I only returned the cards because my grandmother made me. Otherwise I would have thrown them in the garbage. I don't like people who miss appointments."

Tod chuckled. "So there was an appointment was there? Interesting."

"There was no appointment," I said.

Ollie gave me a fiery look, then turned and strode away.

Tod shoved me. "What's wrong with you? A girl comes all the way down here to see you, and you treat her like that? She's pretty, too, let me tell you." He gave me another shove that nearly knocked me off my feet. "Go on, go talk to her."

"Aye, tell her to never show herself around here again," Nucky muttered, counting the money he had in his pockets. "I did a good deal on those spoons. What does she know? Damned busybody."

"Clay? Wake Up!" Tod gave me a slap on the back that winded me. "Either you run after her or I will."

"I'm going, I'm going," I grumbled. "Hey, Ollie! Wait a minute!"

Needless to say, she didn't turn but kept walking away across Blackfriars Bridge at an even faster pace. In spite of myself, I found myself running after her. "Wait!"

If it hadn't been for a tram almost running her over, Ollie wouldn't have stopped and I wouldn't have been able to catch up with her. I grabbed her by the arm. "Ollie . . ."

She wriggled free. "You really are a—"

"Get out of the way, you brats!" barked a carriage driver, swinging his whip in the air.

I jumped aside, pushing myself up against the railing of the bridge to avoid being run over by the horses. Ollie, though, gave the man a rude gesture and shouted a barrage of incomprehensible words after him. It was probably the curse I'd narrowly escaped earlier.

With a nimble leap, Ollie sat down on the railing. Perhaps she was willing to talk after all. I sat down beside her, just as a barge loaded up with barrels passed lazily below us, steered by a man singing at the top of his lungs, "Greensleeves was my delight. Greensleeves, my heart of gold. Greensleeves was my heart of joy!"

"How gross," Ollie said with a look of disgust. "Whoever wrote that must be a real sissy."

"So you don't know who wrote it?" I asked.

"No. You do?"

I nodded. "Henry VIII. For Anne Boleyn, his second wife. Before he had her head chopped off. Not exactly how a sissy acts."

Ollie suddenly looked surprised. "How do you know all this?"

"I was brought up by a mud lark with a passion for history and books," I answered.

"So you can read?"

"Aye."

"Lucky you," sighed Ollie. "My grandmother never wanted

to teach me. She says that all I need to be able to read is tarot cards."

"By the way . . . thank you for bringing them back. And I'm sorry about what I said yesterday," I quickly added. "I don't really want you to be eaten by circus animals."

"But that's what you said," Ollie answered.

"Well, you were defending Parson and his son!" I complained.

"Are you sure?" Ollie asked. "If I remember correctly, you ran away before I could explain."

I realized she was right. "So you don't think like them?"

"Clay, I'm a didicoy. My grandmother's been around the world twice. I was conceived in Germany, born in England, and lived in Romania with my father's paternal family until I was six. If there's one thing I could never do, is spend my life locked in a cage. So, no, I don't like the way Parson and Hiram treat the animals. I don't like seeing them suffer. I don't like seeing their freedom taken away." She shrugged, fiddling with the countless bracelets on her wrists. "But my grandmother is very old, and this circus is our only way to survive. The truth is, without the tigers, bears, and monkeys, we wouldn't make any money. They're the main attractions, definitely not the trapeze artists or jugglers or us fortune tellers. And now we have the wolf, all the newspapers are talking about us. Even Queen Victoria is coming to see him. It's going to be raining money."

I stayed silent, thinking over Ollie's words. I had to admit that I'd judged her too quickly. After all, she was like me and did what she had to do to survive.

"But why is Hiram so horrible to the animals?" I asked, thinking about his sadistic gaze.

Ollie shook her head. "He's always been like that, even when he was a child, even before he started helping his father in the menagerie. He used to torture mice, frogs, and other small animals."

"But why?"

"Because the only way he can feel good about himself is by making others feel bad."

"He must not have a very happy life."

"No, but it's what he's chosen for himself," replied Ollie.

"I guess he hasn't got a lot of friends in the circus."

"On the contrary," Ollie answered, "he's the leader of his gang. They call themselves the Daredevil Gang."

"It's not a great name," I commented. "It doesn't sound very good. The Terrors of Blackfriars Bridge sounds much better."

Ollie didn't seem impressed. She obviously thought both names were ridiculous.

"Are you part of the gang, too?" I asked.

"Don't be silly! I don't want anything to do with those idiots. They're all terrified of my grandmother. They say she's a witch."

I didn't ask Ollie if that was true, because I didn't really want to know the answer. I brought the conversation back to the wolf.

"Do the circus owners know what Parson and Hiram are like?"

"Of course. Smith and Sparrow are even crueler than they are. Animals are just a source of money for them. And when an animal's too old to perform, they think it's useless and they put it down."

I was speechless for a moment. "They put it down?" I repeated.

"Yes," Ollie said grimly.

"So that will happen to the wolf, too?" I said bitterly. "After he spends the rest of his life behind bars?"

Ollie nodded. "His home is hundreds of miles from here, up north. Anyway"—she leapt down off the railing and dusted off her dress—"once Parson and Hiram have tamed him, Smith and Sparrow will treat him as kindly as you like. That animal's going to be a goldmine."

"What if Parson and Hiram can't tame him?" I asked.

Ollie stared at me. "An animal that can't perform is useless, Clay. And useless animals . . ."

I knew what she was going to say. At Smith & Sparrow's Amazing Circus, useless animals get slaughtered.

FOUR

I went to the circus that evening.

The sun had set some time before, and the scarlet tent glowed in the flickering light of torches and bonfires. I climbed over the fence, avoided being spotted by the watchmen on horseback, quickly slipped between two wagons, and hid among the shadows.

Some women were dancing to a drum around a bonfire, waving their colorful shawls in the air. A little farther on, a man with his body covered in blue tattoos was sharpening the long blade of a sword on a stone.

"I thought you were done with this place." A voice surprised me from behind.

I turned, taking my attention away from the tattooed man. "Not yet."

Ollie waited for me to explain.

"I'm going to set the wolf free," I said.

I was ready to have to face up to Ollie protesting, but all she did was shrug. "I know," she said simply.

"You know?"

"My grandmother saw that you were going to make up your mind to free the wolf. In the cards."

"Oh," I murmured. "Did she also see if he'll kill me?"

"No," said Ollie, "but I don't think you need a didicoy to work that out."

"Is it that obvious?"

"You want to free a ferocious beast that sees humans as its greatest enemy. How do you think it will end?"

"The only way it could."

Ollie smiled. "At least you realize."

"Not much of a consolation." I stared at the leaping flames of the nearby bonfire. "I know you don't want to help me, but at least please don't try to stop me. That's all I ask."

"Sorry, but when did I say that?"

"What?"

"That I don't want to help you."

I looked at her without understanding. "But what about

this circus being the only way you and your grandmother have to survive?"

"I told you, I don't like the way Parson and Hiram treat the animals," she said quickly, "and I am willing to help you, but only without risking my place here. If you get caught, you're on your own."

I studied Ollie for a long moment. "You've got a strange way of thinking, you know."

"Says the river kid who's decided to free a mountain wolf."

I smiled. Ollie was full of contradictions but she did want to help me, and that was good enough for me. "Well, thank you, then."

"Don't thank me yet," she warned. "I'll say it again: if things go badly, you're on your own."

I nodded. "Seems fair."

I held out my hand. With a look full of distrust, she squeezed it.

⁂

Even though there had never been any secrets between us, I decided not to tell Tod and Nucky. To explain my sudden interest in Smith & Sparrow's Amazing Circus, I let them think that Ollie and I were sweet on each other. Considering her attitude to me, though, nothing could have been further from the truth.

"Good for you, Clay!" Tod said when I announced next morning that I was going to the circus that night to see Ollie.

"Who knows what Old Sal will think." Nucky grinned.

"Aye," I murmured as I continued to dig in the mud with an absorbed air.

I'd even decided not to tell Old Sal what I was up to. What could I have said? "Hey, Sal, you know that the lad you raised as your own son has decided to go off and get mauled by a wolf? And the funniest thing is that you convinced him to do it!"

It was out of the question.

At the end of that long day, I stopped at the Smithfield meat market on my way to the circus. It was a horrible place, dirty and filled with a nauseating stench. While Tod and I refused to set foot in the place (partly because we hardly ever had the money to afford meat), Nucky, needless to say, had no problem going there. Actually, I'd gotten the idea that the market was his main source of inspiration for his gruesome stories about the Great Stink of '58.

I wandered around the market looking for my victim. I hadn't made this decision lightly. The butchers had a good arsenal of knives, cleavers, and other delightful tools they wouldn't hesitate to use if they had to.

When I saw a particularly old butcher at his counter, I took my place and waited patiently. In that chaos of sounds, noises, and smells, it was only a matter of time until something distracted him. And, a little while later, a dog appeared from who knows where and dived under the counter in search of a bone to gnaw.

"Clear off, you filthy beast!" shouted the angry butcher, chasing him for a few yards. "Clear off!"

I'd never stolen anything in my life—Old Sal wouldn't have stood for it—and I had no plans to start now. All I took were some scraps of pork that the butcher had thrown in a bucket. I wrapped them in a cloth, slipped them into my pocket, and quickly disappeared into the crowd.

I got to the circus just after midnight. Despite the time, the place was still bustling with activity. The performers were gathered around the numerous bonfires and were drinking, eating, and putting on short performances. I was about to sneak between two wagons on my way to the menagerie, when I saw the man with the blue tattoos again. He was sitting on the ground with his back against a crate, a little apart from the rest of them. He was carving a piece of wood with a small knife, pausing from time to time to examine his work.

He was so engrossed in what he was doing that I thought

he hadn't noticed me, when he suddenly looked up right into my eyes. For a moment, I was sure that he'd hand me over to the watchmen, or at least shout that there was an intruder. Instead, after a long moment, he focused back on his work as if nothing had happened.

I decided not to tempt fate again and darted back between the wagons until I got to the menagerie. Ollie was waiting for me, constantly looking around with a worried expression.

"It's about time!" she snapped when she saw me. "The next round is in less than ten minutes!"

"Sorry, but I—"

"*Shh!*" Ollie pulled back the tent flap. "Inside!"

"But it's pitch-dark!" I muttered, peering inside.

"There are oil lamps next to those sacks," Ollie said. "I'll stay here and make sure no one's coming."

I glanced in the direction of the cages. Even though I couldn't see them, I knew the animals were there. I felt them. And I was sure they could feel me. I looked at Ollie. "Are you sure your grandmother didn't tell you if I'm going to be ripped to shreds?"

"Stop joking."

"I'm not."

Ollie sighed in exasperation before glancing over her shoulder. "Clay, if they catch us . . ."

"All right, all right," I muttered. "Here I go."

I plucked up my courage and entered the menagerie. I picked up an oil lamp and lit the wick. The walls of the tent were covered with eerie shadows that swayed with every step I took.

Come on, Clay, I told myself. It's time to prove who you are.

Step by step, I made my way slowly through the menagerie, my heart pounding in my ears.

Tum-tum. Tum-tum. Tum-tum.

When I passed their cage, the lions jerked their heads up, nostrils flaring. They'd smelled blood. And I wasn't sure if it was just the scraps of pork.

Now I know what a worm in a henhouse feels like, I thought.

It wasn't much of an image but it was exactly how I saw myself: small, naked, defenseless, and at the mercy of creatures that were bigger and more dangerous than me.

I stopped a few steps from the wolf's cage, which was again covered by the black tarpaulin.

This is it.

I reached out a trembling hand. I was shaking from head to toe, to tell the truth. Somehow I managed to grip the tarpaulin and started pulling.

"For the love of God!" I muttered as the canvas fell to the ground.

The wolf was waiting for me. He was sitting in the middle of the cage with his big amber eyes staring at me. Despite the dim light, I could make out lighter spots around his nose and mouth, and the arched shape of his ears.

He knows I'm his friend, I thought confidently. Animals feel these things.

"It's all right," I whispered, offering him the pork. "I'm here to help. Not like the other two."

Bam!

It happened in a blink of an eye.

A powerful blow, a ferocious growl, and I found myself upside down in front of that two-hundred-pound silver colossus, its teeth bared, its scarlet gums covered with drool, and its eyes staring as it did everything it could to break out of the cage.

"Clay, come on!" Ollie shouted. "Get out of there!"

"No!" I snapped. "I only have to make him understand that I'm on his side!"

"On his side? You're outside the cage and he's in it! That's the side you're on!" Ollie yelled.

I got up and pushed the scraps of meat back into the cage. "Mist, I'm here to help you," I kept repeating. "You don't need to be af—"

Bam! Bam! Bam!

The bars began creaking.

"He's breaking the bars! He's breaking the bars!" Ollie screamed. "Clay, get out of there! Now!"

"But . . ."

Ollie left her post at the entrance and ran over to me, grabbing my arm as Mist snarled madly, banging his head and paws into the iron bars.

"*Move!*"

Ollie dragged me back toward the exit, while I, feeling dejected and in shock at the wolf's reaction, stared in a daze at the package of pork scraps that had fallen on the ground, a sad symbol of my naivety.

FIVE

"You look awful this morning. Problems with your sweetheart?"

I'd just stepped out of the shack after a sleepless night. Tod and Nucky were eating some leftovers in the sun before they started digging.

I muttered something vague and sat down next to Nucky, while Tod kept grinning at me.

"Here, I think you need it," he said, handing me some bread and cheese.

I gulped down the food almost without tasting it, I was so frustrated by last night's failure. I'd known it wasn't going to be easy but never thought it would go that badly. Mist had lashed out at me with a ferocious, crazy rage, without giving me the slightest chance to prove who I was. Maybe I'd never get him to accept me. And, I thought bitterly, if I couldn't, I'd never be able to save him from Parson and his son.

"Someone looks upset," I heard Tod say. I looked up, not understanding. He pointed to my leg. I was nervously bouncing it up and down.

Annoyed by Tod's and Nucky's half-intrigued, half-amused expressions, I jumped to my feet. "I'm going to sell some stuff at Madame Lorna's," I announced. "I'll be back later."

"Come on, Clay, don't be mad," Nucky yelled after me. "We were only joking!"

I waved at him to say that I wasn't offended and hurried away anxiously.

The night before, after the disaster with Mist, Ollie had insisted on walking me back to the river. Her apparent kindness had an ulterior motive: she tried to make me forget about freeing the wolf.

"Listen, Clay, maybe you should give up now," she said. "You saw how the wolf reacted. How are you going to set him free without being torn to shreds?"

"I still don't know," I answered. "I'll find a way."

Ollie shook her head. "What did you call him? Mist?"

"Aye."

"Why Mist?"

"Because of the color of his fur. And then that's how I imagine the place he comes from: remote, wild, shrouded in mist, and impossible to find."

"Well, obviously it's not that impossible to find, since someone managed to catch him."

Annoyed by Ollie's cynical comment, I'd stayed silent until we saw Blackfriars Bridge.

"I'm here," I said.

"Good," Ollie sighed. "Tomorrow I'll be away all day with my grandmother. We're going to read the cards at a few customers' houses, but if you're really determined to try with Mist again, I'll see you in front of the menagerie before the midnight patrol."

Even though I knew going to the circus in broad daylight without Ollie was a bad idea, I couldn't wait. I had to fix last night's disaster as soon as possible.

When I got to Smith & Sparrow's Amazing Circus, the

surveillance wasn't as tight as usual: the watchmen on horseback were busy breaking up a fight between a pair of knife throwers and some trapeze artists who were unhappy that the knife throwers were using their wagon as a target.

I climbed over the fence and quickly vanished into the general chaos, heading for the menagerie. As I was walking past the wagons with the animals, I heard a voice.

"Just look at it, lads! It's pathetic!"

I stopped. Don't get involved, I told myself straightaway. Go to Mist. He's the reason you're here.

I started walking again, clenching my fists.

"So who wants first shot?"

I stopped again and, after a moment's hesitation, slid between two wagons, following Hiram's voice.

There he is, I thought when I saw him.

Hiram and his gang had surrounded a mangy kitten that looked only a few weeks old. It didn't take a genius to connect the walnut shells glued to its paws and Hiram's grinning face. In turn, the boys started throwing stones at the cat, which cried in terror, unable to escape its tormentors.

"How much do you want to bet I can hit it in the eye?" Hiram exclaimed, taking aim. "Here, you ugly, disgusting beast. I'm going to make you blind as well as lame. . . ."

It was too much.

"Leave that cat alone!" I ordered as I came out from my hiding place.

Hiram lowered the hand holding the stone and looked me up and down. "And who are you? And why should you care about the cat? Is it yours?"

"No, it belongs to the didicoy," I lied. "And if I were you, I wouldn't get her angry."

Just a mention of Ollie's grandmother and Hiram lost some of his brashness. But he wasn't ready to give in yet.

"Well, we haven't done anything to it," he answered boldly. "A bit of a wash and it'll be as good as new." He then added malignantly, "You could do with a bit of a wash, too, mud lark. You stink of slime."

"And you stink of bully," I replied. "Actually, of coward. Why don't you try bullying a cat that's more your own size? The menagerie's full of them. Outside the cage, though."

Hiram dropped his stone. "Coward, hey?" he repeated, rolling up his sleeves with a grin. "You've started a fight with the wrong person, mud lark."

"You, too," I answered.

I was getting ready to fight when Hiram's attention was drawn to something behind me. I turned. The man with the blue tattoos was standing between two wagons, his eyes fixed on Hiram. Without saying a word, he walked past me and picked up the kitten. When he bent down, the huge eye tattooed on his back seemed to open wide.

Under the frightened gaze of everyone—mine, too, I don't deny it—he hugged the cat in one arm and turned to Hiram. "Hiram," he said in a cold voice, "your father wants you in the menagerie."

Realizing it was time to retreat, Hiram shot me a look that said that this wasn't finished here. Then he motioned to his gang, and everyone hurried after him.

I was about to slip away, too, when the tattooed man nailed me with his icy gaze. "Be careful of Hiram, river boy," he said. "You're not like him."

"I know."

"Then don't behave like him."

And, without another word, he left.

Once, when I was nine, I decided that I was going to pull a wagon wheel out of the mud of the river. I don't know why I cared so much about the wheel or what I was even going to do with it, but I spent hours pulling and pulling, with nothing to show for it but swollen hands, covered in cuts and splinters.

When he'd come home that night, Old Sal had found me on the front steps in tears. He'd sat silently next to me and, after filling his pipe, looked at me. "Why are you crying, Clay?"

"I . . . I wanted to pull the wheel out of the mud," I sobbed. "But I couldn't do it."

"Just because you didn't succeed today doesn't mean you won't succeed tomorrow."

"B-but it's too heavy!" I'd protested. "I . . . I pulled it with all the strength I have, but it won't move an inch!"

With his pipe, Sal had pointed at the wheel, half buried in the hard, dry mud. "What do you see, Clay?"

"What do you mean what do I see? A wooden wheel. Actually, no. Half a wheel. The other half is under the mud."

"Exactly," Old Sal had said. "That's the half you need to think about. The one you can't see."

Old Sal had ruffled my hair and then went into the house, leaving me to ponder his strange statement.

The next morning, at first light of dawn, I left the house armed with a long iron nail. I sat down next to the wheel and began digging around it with a stone, clearing away the mud an inch at a time.

It had taken me almost a week, but in the end I got what I wanted. All I had to do was look at the problem from a different angle.

And that's just what I needed to do with Mist.

That evening, the circus opened to the enthusiastic London audience. Rivers of people poured into the open space near Westminster Bridge, eager for their share of the awe and wonder. Many of them, I was sure, were hoping to get a peek at the Wild Beast of the North before the show on July 17, tickets for which were now as rare as hen's teeth.

When I got to the circus, I found the entire perimeter lit up by dozens and dozens of flickering torches. From the scarlet tent came shouting, music, and applause, as knots of ticketless onlookers crowded near the entrance, being kept under control by the mounted watchmen. With all that going on, it was easy for me to get to the menagerie unnoticed.

I found Ollie waiting for me. She was wearing a long golden dress, while her face was covered in cosmetics. "Don't say a thing," she warned me with a dark look.

"I wouldn't dream of it," I answered.

"Just as well," she said, throwing back the flap to the menagerie.

I hurried in and was immediately greeted by the now

familiar stench of the animals, even though most of the cages were empty that evening.

"The crowd went crazy over the pig jugglers," said Ollie. "They asked for two encores. Could anyone be more stupid?"

"Probably," I muttered as I sat down on the ground.

"What are you doing?" Ollie asked with a puzzled look. "Why are you sitting here? The wolf's over there."

"I know, but I'm not going to go to him."

"You think you can convince him that you're his friend by sitting here and doing nothing?"

"Exactly. Now shut up, please. You're disturbing us."

Ollie closed the flap, while muttering the usual string of incomprehensible words, and left me alone with the wolf.

As soon as he saw me, Mist jumped to his feet, his ears and tail erect, and his muzzle straight. He gave me a low, menacing growl.

I didn't react. I stayed where I was, motionless, without trying to communicate with him.

Ten minutes later, when Ollie warned me that the patrol was about to go by, both Mist and I were in exactly the same positions as when she'd left us.

"Suit yourself," she said, unconvinced. "I don't understand what you hope to achieve like this."

"You'll see."

For seven nights, I sat in front of Mist's cage in silence, moving a few inches closer each time. For seven nights, he reacted to my presence with his menacing growl. For seven nights, I ignored Ollie's skeptical gaze and whispered comments.

Then, on the eighth night, something changed.

When I entered the menagerie, I wasn't greeted by the usual growl. Lying on the bottom of the cage, Mist simply lifted his head and looked at me. Then, when I sat down on the ground in front of him, he put his muzzle back down on his paws, but without taking his eyes off me.

I turned and responded to Ollie's astonished gaze with a smile. It had worked. The wolf had finally accepted my presence. From then on, it was going to be easier.

"Why are you in such a good mood?" Nucky asked the evening after as we were walking back to the shack for dinner. "You've been whistling all day. And you never whistle, Clay."

"Because he doesn't know how," said Tod. "It sounds like someone strangling a bird."

I answered my friends' comments with a laugh. My

whistle was quite awful, but I was so happy with what I'd achieved the night before with Mist that I couldn't help it. I'd been in a good mood all day. So much so that when some unknown mud lark crossed over into our territory, I'd convinced Tod and Nucky to let him pass by without doing anything to him.

"Old Sal!" Nucky exclaimed happily when he saw him waiting for us at the front door. "I bet he's got something for us to eat."

"Hello, Sal," I greeted him.

"Lads," he said, putting a full sack down on the floor.

Nucky pounced on the sack and opened it. "Bread! Cheese! And . . . my God, kidney pie!"

I grinned at Old Sal. "The maid in Kensington again?"

He answered with a raised eyebrow and walked away, his pipe in his mouth, his hands in his pockets.

"That man is a true gentleman," Nucky said, his eyes sparkling. "You were very lucky to be adopted by him."

I couldn't have agreed more. Old Sal hadn't just saved my life by feeding me and putting a roof over my head, he'd helped me discover the world and taught me the difference between right and wrong.

And that's why I felt so guilty. I should have told him about Mist, but I couldn't. I was afraid of what he'd say. I was afraid that, despite his words, he wouldn't understand.

My two associates and I gorged ourselves and, at about eleven o'clock, while they lay snoring on the straw mattresses, I slipped out of the shack and headed for Smith & Sparrow's Amazing Circus.

After my recent success, I was full of expectation for my meeting with Mist. Obviously, I didn't think the wolf would let me stroke him or anything like that, but I was sure that, with a little patience, I would be able to get closer and closer to him.

But when I saw the expression on Ollie's face as she waited for me by the entrance to the menagerie, I knew right away that things weren't going to go the way I'd hoped. "What's wrong?" I asked, trying to pull back the tent flap.

She held me by the arm. "Tonight isn't a good idea."

"Why? What's going on?"

"Clay, just trust me."

"Let me go, Ollie!"

"No, wait!"

I struggled and pushed her aside. I flung open the tent flap, lit one of the oil lamps, and lifted it over my head.

"Oh no. . . . Mist . . ."

I hardly had enough time to see the hideous burn on his side before the wolf thew himself toward me, growling furiously, his scarlet gums dripping with drool.

"Mist, it's me!" I exclaimed. What had those two done to him? How could they hurt him like that? "It's me!"

But Mist wasn't listening. What little I'd painstakingly achieved with calm, respect, and patience after days and days of work had been swept away in a matter of hours by the trainer and his son. I left the menagerie in a rage and threw the lamp on the ground.

"Clay . . ."

Ollie tried to stop me, but she couldn't. No one could have. I was burning with anger, frustration, and a need for justice. I walked past the animal wagons to the bonfire area. It was busier than usual that night, with noisy groups of artists performing, singing, and drinking. I saw Hiram with a couple of the kids from his gang and headed straight for them.

"Hiram!" I called to him.

He turned with an annoyed expression. But when he recognized me, he grinned. "You're brave, mud lark. What have you made up your mind to—"

Before he could finish the sentence, I gave him a shove. Hiram fell over, but more from surprise than the force of the push. Without giving him time to figure out what had happened, I jumped on him, grabbing him by the shirt.

After a moment of shock, his two friends threw themselves

on us, too, partly to break us up, partly to punch me. In an instant, we were surrounded by dozens of onlookers.

"Get him off me, you idiots!" Hiram shouted. "Get him off me!"

But I had no intention of letting him go. All I could think of was Mist's wounded body and the hate for my species in his eyes. Hiram had to pay for what he'd done to the wolf and the other animals in the menagerie. Someone had to punish him. Someone had to make him stop. And I'd decided that that someone was me.

Two strong hands grabbed me by the shoulders, and before I knew it, I was yards away from Hiram.

"In God's name . . . ," I began, turning to see who it was holding me back. "You?" I exclaimed when I met the icy gaze of the man with the blue tattoos. I tried to free myself, but his hands were like vices. "Let me go!"

He ignored me and, despite my protests, began to drag me away.

Meanwhile, Hiram was back on his feet and rubbing his face. "Run, mud lark, run! But there won't always be someone to protect you! Sooner or later, I'll catch you alone!"

"I hope so!" I yelled back, frustrated at not being able to avenge Mist. "I'm Clay from Blackfriars Bridge! Come and look for me at the river. I'll be waiting for you!"

SIX

"Well done. Besides telling him your name and where to find you, did you also mention what you're doing at the circus every night?" Ollie was furious.

I muttered something vague as I pressed a poultice to my cheek. Nucky had made it for me when he'd woken up and found me collapsed on my mattress with a battered face. The poultice smelled disgusting, to say the least, but knowing Nucky's hygiene habits, it could have been worse.

"Here it is!" he'd announced, happy on his return from collecting the ingredients. "Clay, gull poop, and a couple of fresh shellfish."

"Whoever did that to you has made a big mistake," said

Tod grimly. "You don't lay a finger on one of the Terrors of Blackfriars Bridge without having to deal with the other two."

"Hear, hear, Tod!" said Nucky as he smeared the disgusting mixture on my face. "The three of us are one."

Feeling very guilty about the lies I'd been telling my two friends for days, I dismissed what they were saying with a wave. "No one did anything to me. I fell like an idiot when I was climbing over the circus fence."

As for Nucky's concoction, I had to admit it worked. The pain in my cheek was slowly subsiding. Or maybe I was about to pass out from the stink. It was difficult to say.

"Sorry, what was that? I didn't hear you," Ollie growled with her hands on her hips.

Her anger was more than justified: I'd been an idiot to expose myself that way to the circus people. Now everyone— or at least everyone who saw the fight between Hiram and me—knew who I was. Not getting noticed during my nighttime visits was now going to be much more difficult.

"I said I'm sorry," I mumbled, looking at Ollie apologetically. We were sitting outside my shack on an old millstone. No one had any idea how it had got there.

"Look, if Parson starts to suspect anything, he'll put the wolf in solitary confinement," Ollie threatened. "And then I won't be able to help you anymore."

"Hiram hasn't worked anything out. He's too stupid."

"Maybe, but you're the one who tried to fight three boys bigger than you."

"I didn't know that courage was something to be ashamed of."

"Courage, no. Stupidity, yes," Ollie said. "But I wonder why Asher got involved," she then mused out loud. "He usually lives like a hermit and doesn't meddle in other people's affairs."

I had an idea what the explanation was. After reluctantly promising Ollie that I'd stay away from the circus for a couple of days, I left my shack and went to see Old Sal.

He was sitting on an old, overturned boat in front of his house, smoking his pipe, and gazing at the glistening water of the river.

I sat down next to him. "I met your friend with the blue tattoos."

He took his pipe out of his mouth. "Interesting gentleman, don't you think?"

I had to laugh. "Sal, how is it that you always know everything?"

"It's a privilege of old men."

"You're not that old, Sal." I eyed him closely. "At least, I don't think you are."

We sat in silence for a while. My head was full of questions, but it was always like that with Old Sal.

"There's something I don't understand," I finally said. "Why don't you try to stop me?"

"Why should I?" he replied. "You made a choice, Clay, and I have to respect it."

"I could get hurt."

"All choices have consequences."

"Aye, but we're talking about getting torn to pieces."

Old Sal gave me one of his rare smiles. "It won't happen."

"Thanks for your trust," I muttered. "But I'm not so sure anymore. Maybe I'm doing everything wrong."

"You know, Clay, making mistakes is the privilege of people who've had the courage to take action. People who don't do anything have nothing but a fantasy that they could have done better."

That evening, lying on my straw mattress with Tod and Nucky snoring beside me, I thought long and hard about Old Sal's words and realized that I couldn't lose heart and leave Mist to his fate. I'd have to try everything to save him, no matter what it cost me.

"Aren't you going to the circus tonight?"

Nucky and I were sitting by the river, cleaning a walking stick with a silver knob that we'd found under the bridge that morning.

"Just another rich man too drunk to hold on to his treasures," Tod said scornfully, and then walked off to the Whitechapel Market to buy food.

"Well?" Nucky pressed me in my silence. "Did you have a fight with Ollie? That doesn't surprise me. She's such a know-it-all."

I chuckled. Nucky would never forgive her for criticizing his way of doing business. "I'm seeing her tonight," I answered.

Despite his dislike of Ollie, Nucky, like a good friend, smiled at me. "Good for you."

I was silent for a moment, not knowing what to do. Lying was becoming too hard. "Nucky . . ."

He broke a big chunk of dried mud off the silver knob and cheered. "Hallelujah!" Then he looked at me. "Well?"

I shook my head. "Nothing, nothing."

He shrugged, too excited by our treasure to ask questions.

After we'd finished cleaning the walking stick, we scoured the bank for some promising spot to start digging. Over the last few days, the river had been quite generous and had given us lots of interesting objects.

"What the devil . . . ?" I muttered when I saw Tod in the distance. "Tod!" I called. "What happened?"

"For the love of God," Nucky muttered.

Tod came over to us with one hand pressed on a swollen, bleeding lip. "The Tower Hounds," he explained, throwing the sack of food from the market onto the ground. "You'd better enjoy it, because it almost cost me a tooth defending it."

"You trespassed onto their territory?" I asked, surprised. The Tower Hounds were an especially vicious and big group of mud larks who'd taken over the river near the old prison. We kept well away from them.

"Of course not," he answered. "They're not just on the north bank anymore, but on the south, too. As well as some of the streets to the market."

"But they can't!" Nucky exclaimed. "That's against the rules!"

Tod shrugged. "They've joined up with a gang of pickpockets who hang out around Whitechapel and hunt down the other mud larks."

Nucky swore and poked his head into the sack. He pulled out an apple and took a bite. "We can't do nothing," he said. "We have to react. I say we wait for it to get dark and then go and pay them back. Clay, what do you think?"

I looked at my two associates doubtfully. "It doesn't sound

like a good idea to me." It obviously wasn't, but the main reason I didn't want them to carry out their plan for revenge was Mist. I wanted to see him as soon as I could, and try to undo the damage done by Parson and Hiram. I didn't have time to fight with the Hounds.

"Heck, Clay, but they punched one of us!" Nucky exclaimed in outrage.

I couldn't help thinking about their reaction when they'd found me in bed with a battered face. Before even knowing what had happened, they were ready to take revenge.

"Clay," Nucky urged. "Do you really want to stand here doing nothing?"

"I . . ."

"No, he's right," said Tod. "It's not worth starting a war over something so little. I'll have a swim and will be as good as new." Tod limped off toward our shack.

After a few moments and a puzzled look, Nucky stood up. "You know, Clay, if I didn't know you better, I'd almost say you couldn't care less about what happened to Tod." He then hoisted the sack onto his shoulder and walked away, leaving me alone with my guilt.

With the mounted watchmen patrolling and more or less everyone at the circus now knowing my face, it was pretty unlikely I'd go unnoticed if I climbed over the fence. So I met Ollie over by the elephant yard instead, which bordered an old brick wall. She was waiting for me, sitting on a full hay cart and holding an oil lamp.

"So how's Mist?" I asked as soon as I saw her. "Is he still angry?"

Ollie shook her head and jumped down off the wagon. "Worse."

"What could be worse?" I asked anxiously, as she led me past the elephants tied to poles. They were so big they could have crushed me with a foot, but they didn't seem interested in us at all and just kept swinging their tails lazily to shoo away insects.

"You'll see," she replied grimly.

When we reached the menagerie, Ollie stood on lookout at the entrance, while I slipped through the flap, impatient to find out what was going on. I was ready for anything. I was ready for a furious animal. I was ready for an animal thirsting for revenge. I was ready for an animal full of hatred for people.

Instead, I found an animal that had decided to stop fighting. A defeated animal. Resigned to his fate. A shadow of what he'd been.

Mist lay on the bottom of the cage with his eyes open, but he didn't seem to see what was around him. The burn on his side had been treated, but there was another wound, an invisible wound, which wouldn't be so easy to heal.

When I got nearer, he just gave me a blank look.

Ollie, who'd hardly ever dared to leave the entrance to the menagerie, came and joined me with no fear. "He's been like this for two days. He refuses to eat or leave his cage. Parson and Hiram drag him out, but then he just lies on the ground and doesn't move."

"Mist . . . ," I whispered.

"Smith and Sparrow are getting nervous," Ollie added. "It's only five days until Mist's debut, and if Parson and Hiram haven't trained him—"

"I know," I interrupted. "They'll say Mist is a useless animal." And we both knew what that meant.

"I told that good-for-nothing Parson that he has three days."

Ollie spun around toward the entrance. "Smith!" she exclaimed.

"Three days is already too long. He's been wasting time for weeks."

Ollie turned pale. "Sparrow!" She took my hand. "Come on! We've got to hide!" She blew out the oil lamp and dragged me behind some crates. We crouched there for a moment before the two circus owners stepped into the tent.

Of all the horrible people I'd come across in my thirteen years of life (and I had met quite a few, believe me), Smith and Sparrow were definitely at the top of the list. They were both in their fifties and there was a gaudy look about them, with that combination of clothes and accessories typical of someone who's made too much money too quickly.

Smith was short, stocky, and had greasy, combed-back red hair. He wore a purple satin top hat, a jacket with tails, and a bright green scarf. Sparrow was a little taller but just as stocky. He was completely bald and had heavy-lidded eyes, wore a dozen pocket watches on gold chains and had a ridiculous yellow silk handkerchief with red polka dots. Both had walking sticks made of dark wood with inlaid silver handles.

"So what do you suggest we do?" asked Smith, walking over to Mist's cage. He waved his cane at the wolf in contempt. "Look how disgusting it is. And think of all the money we paid that hunter."

"Let's skin it and sell the skin," suggested Sparrow. "It would be worth a lot of money."

"And what about all those posters? All of London is expecting the fat woman to come to the show."

I looked at Ollie, not understanding. "The fat woman?" I mouthed.

"The queen," she mouthed back.

I gasped. Not that Queen Victoria had ever had any interest in us mud larks, but she was still the queen. Insulting her like that was a disgrace.

"And so?" asked Smith, banging his walking stick against the bars. "Wake up, fleabag! Wake up, damn you!"

"We'll give Parson two days," Sparrow said. "If he doesn't get any results in two days, we'll kick him and his feral son out of the circus."

"And what will we do with this animal?"

Sparrow shrugged. "We could let the audience lynch it. Crowds love blood, you know. We could find someone who's missing an arm or leg, say that they were attacked by the wolf, and then ask the public to deliver justice. They'll love it. You'll see."

I was horrified. Smith and Sparrow were the real animals. Human animals with no compassion or pity.

"Keep calm," Ollie warned me, squeezing my hand. "Keep calm, Clay."

Smith and Sparrow left the tent, talking about lynching Mist as if it were just another part of the show.

I jumped to my feet, walked over to the wolf's cage, and

knelt down. "Mist," I said. "Get up. Please get up. Did you hear those two? They'll kill you if you just lie there like that!"

The wolf stayed where he was, indifferent to my words and my closeness.

"Clay, I don't think he's listening," said Ollie. "Anyway, even if he was, he wouldn't understand. He's an animal. There's no point talking to him like you'd talk to a person."

I ignored her comment. I was sure that Mist understood perfectly what was happening around him.

"Do you think they were serious?" I asked Ollie. "Would they really have him lynched by the audience?"

She nodded confidently. "The newspapers would talk about it for months. It would be great advertising for them."

"But they can't kill an animal like that!"

Ollie shook her head. "Clay, you sometimes seem so naive for someone who grew up on the street. What about dog fights? Half of London bets on dog fights."

I looked back at Mist. I had to do something, but I didn't know what. And I only had two days. Two days before the wolf, one way or another, would be sentenced to death.

SEVEN

I spent the night lying on the ground in front of Mist's cage. I woke up just before dawn, sore and with my temples throbbing. Mist hadn't moved since the night before and was lying on his side, still staring at nothing.

If I don't do anything, Parson and Hiram will torture him, especially now that Smith and Sparrow are planning to pressure them, I thought desperately.

"Mist," I called to him. "Please. Do something. Damn, do something!"

The wolf didn't move or react.

"Do you want to die?" I stood up. "Is that what you want? Because that's what's going to happen!" I yelled, kicking the cage.

The panther and lions paced nervously around their cages, annoyed by my screams, but I got no reaction from Mist.

"Well, you know what? You might be ready to give up, but I'm not."

I began rolling up my sleeves. Just then, I heard something move behind me. I spun around, ready to confront Parson or Hiram. To tell the truth, part of me was hoping it was one of them. Instead, I found a sleepy-looking Ollie, wrapped in a long, black fringed shawl.

When she saw me, though, she quickly woke up. "What are you doing here?" she exclaimed. "I thought you left last night!"

"For that matter, what are you doing here?"

"My grandmother," she replied, throwing her hands in the air. "She had one of her premonitions in a dream. Something about a seagull flying over the river in search of a place to land. . . . She didn't give me much of an explanation, but sent me here to check. I was sure that for once she was wrong, but, as usual . . . Sorry, but what do you think you're doing?" She stopped and stared at my bare arm.

"Showing Mist that I'm not like the men she's known."

"You're not going to poke your arm in there, are you?"

"Yes."

"He'll tear it off!"

"Well, at least it will mean that there's something left of the old wolf," I said.

"Clay, please," Ollie begged. "We'll find some way, but it can't be this!"

I looked at her. "Did the seagull in the dream end up with a broken wing?"

Despite herself, Ollie laughed. "You're completely mad."

"Sounds good. Make sure they put that on my gravestone."

With my heart pounding in my ears, I began to put my hand very slowly through the bars of the cage. With his space being invaded, Mist lifted his head and bared his teeth.

A reaction! I thought.

"Oh, God!" exclaimed Ollie, who didn't share my enthusiasm at all. "I can't look!"

Neither could I. So I closed my eyes. I had no idea what Mist was going to do, but I had to show him that I wasn't like Parson and Hiram. I had to show him that a human hand could do more than just inflict pain.

For a very long moment, nothing happened. I stood there, paralyzed. Then something wet touched the back of my hand. Behind me, I heard Ollie stifle a cry.

Then, nothing.

I waited a few seconds before opening my eyes. Mist was

no longer lying on the bottom of the cage. He was now sitting and staring at me, his amber eyes fixed on mine.

He was going to fight back. I knew it. We were going to fight together.

Old Sal always said that to live by the river, you have to learn to hear its voice. I never understood what he meant—well, not really—but that night in late June, despite myself and for the umpteenth time, I felt grateful for my adoptive father and the precious lessons he'd taught me. Because, in a way I could never explain, he had taught me to hear the voice of the river.

I suddenly opened my eyes. The air was humid and heavy. Even though I couldn't see them, I heard Tod and Nucky breathing as they lay on the straw mattresses next to me. Tod's breath was regular and heavy; Nucky's was nasal and restless.

I sat up and stayed motionless for a few moments, just listening. The night noises were the same as always—distant bells, flowing water, echoes of some drunken brawl. And yet . . .

"Tod, Nucky," I called as I stood up. "Wake up."

Nucky moaned something vague, while Tod answered me

immediately with an alert voice. "What's going on, Clay?"

"I don't know," I answered, walking toward the door. "But we'd better take a look."

London was illuminated by a full moon. The banks of the river were dotted with the bonfires of mud larks and beggars, and I could hear drums in the distance. A couple of boats slid lazily under the bridge, laden with crates and barrels.

Tod stood by my side, while Nucky walked over to us, scratching his head sleepily. "What's wrong? Did a ship sink? Is there stuff we can salvage?"

I shook my head and kept gazing at the water. Something was about to happen. The river looked menacing that night. Despite the moon, its water didn't sparkle but ran dark.

Tod grabbed my arm, pulling my attention away from the Thames. "What the hell are those?"

I followed his gaze. Like a swarm of dancing fireflies, torches were moving toward us.

"Oh no. That's all we need," I murmured as I recognized Hiram and his gang.

"Do you know them, Clay?" Nucky asked. "They're not mud larks."

"No, they're not," I answered. "They're from the circus. A while back, I had a disagreement with the big one."

Tod started rolling up his sleeves, while Nucky picked up a stick from the ground. Yet again, my two friends were going to fight for me, no questions asked. Their loyalty made me feel even more guilty about my recent behavior.

They deserve to know the truth, I thought.

"Tod, Nucky, wait. Maybe I can talk our way out of this," I started saying. At that moment, though, Hiram shouted, "Mud larks! Let's get them!"

"Maybe not," I sighed.

Hiram and his gang stopped a few yards from us, legs apart and bristling for a fight. Except for Hiram, the other boys had painted their faces red and white, like terrifying clowns.

"Look, clowns," Tod began with his typical peacemaking approach. "We'll give you ten seconds to get off our territory. After that, you'll regret ever having set foot here."

"We want him," Hiram said, pointing at me. "We're not interested in you or that other one."

"Well, I'm sorry," said Nucky, stepping forward and brandishing his stick, "but the three of us are one. So, if you want Clay, you'll have to deal with us first."

"Boys . . . ," I started, trying to calm the situation. They outnumbered us, and I didn't want Tod and Nucky to get hurt because of me.

"*Charge!*" Hiram shouted.

"*Argh!*" Tod thundered, lunging forward.

It only took me a few seconds to work out that the Daredevil Gang were like their leader: good at bullying those who couldn't defend themselves.

Tod, Nucky, and I had cut our teeth by the river, and we'd often fought people bigger than us. It had always been a question of survival. It certainly wasn't fun or a way to make ourselves feel important. These brats from the circus, though, had never had to struggle to eat or make it to the next day.

"You'd better leave now," Tod said after knocking a couple of them over.

Furious, Hiram rushed at me. We ended up on the ground, rolling about in the mud and trying to get the better of each other.

"You're dead, mud lark!" Hiram snarled.

"I really don't think so," I answered.

"Clay!" I heard someone calling.

"This isn't the time, Tod!" I replied, pounding Hiram into the ground.

"*Clay!*"

I turned my attention away from Hiram, who took the opportunity to push me off him. "Damn, Tod, your timing is—" I began to say, but my friend pulled me to my feet by my shirt.

"Look there."

I followed his gaze and . . .

"Factory men!" Hugging one of the Southwark Bridge lampposts, a mud lark was shouting and waving his hands, "Factory men!"

"Everyone stay still!" I exclaimed in a choked voice. Ignoring my warning, Hiram tried to keep on fighting but soon found himself facing Tod.

"You'd better listen to my friend."

"What the hell?!" Hiram began to protest, but I signaled to him to shut up. In an instant, the rest of his gang were paralyzed by fear and confusion.

"Tod, can you see them?" I whispered.

Before he could answer, we heard cries for help from the other side of the bridge.

"The Scabby Dogs!" Nucky yelled. "They're coming this way!"

Chaos broke out in an instant. Led by the Blonde, the Scabby Dogs crossed into our territory, pursued by about twenty men from the factories armed with sticks. At the same time, four barges docked and another twenty or so men poured out onto the shore. We were surrounded.

"Run!" I screamed. "Run! Run!"

Hiram and the circus brats started running but they had

no idea what was going on. A couple of them, the skinniest ones, were immediately captured and dragged off to the barges.

"Know any good hiding places?" I turned. It was the Blonde.

"Oh! They've given you a real beating," Tod commented, looking at her.

"Shut up, unless you really want your ear cut off this time," she said. But Tod was right: the Blonde was limping, had a gash on her arm, and her face was bruised. She was holding the hand of an eight-year-old boy I'd never seen before. "So do you know any good hiding places or not?" she quickly repeated.

I owed her a favor, so I nodded. "The fisherman's wharf," I whispered. "Follow us."

Tod, Nucky, the Blonde, the boy, and I silently made our way along the riverbank toward the dock. There, between the seaweed-encrusted poles, we kept a little boat that had once belonged to Old Sal. Once on board, we could escape over the river and wait for the men from the factories to go back where they'd come from.

"They came out of nowhere," the Blonde said. "Our lookouts on the bridge didn't see a thing."

"Bastards," Tod muttered.

"Can Old Sal do anything?" Nucky asked.

"No," I answered as we crawled through the mud. "He once tried, but they only care about their damned factories. You can't even bribe them. Here we are. Get in the water one at a time."

The first to go out was Tod, who helped the Blonde and the little boy.

"You go now, Nucky," I whispered as I kept an eye on what was going on behind us. From what I could see, the men from the factories were starting to retreat, dragging away several prisoners with them.

"Damn them," Nucky swore as he climbed into the boat.

Using an oar, Tod took us out from the shore and, within seconds, we were in the middle of the river.

"Keep clear of the barges," I whispered. We were small and silent enough that, with a little luck, they wouldn't spot us.

I turned to the Blonde. "How many of you did they take?"

"Four," she answered. She put a hand on the boy's head. "They almost got him, too."

"Who is he?" asked Tod.

"My brother, Kid," answered the Blonde.

"I didn't know you had a brother," I said.

"He doesn't usually live with me," she explained. "He lives with our grandmother in Whitechapel, but she's sick."

We all kept quiet as the current swept us along the river to safety. The factory men's barges were now far enough away that we started to feel safe. I thought about the children they'd captured. I wanted to do something for them, but I couldn't put our group in danger. The life of a mud lark was hard. We couldn't let ourselves be weak if we were to survive. We couldn't let feelings—

The boat suddenly rocked violently, as if it had run into something.

I clung to the side. "But what the . . . Hey!" A factory man, in the water and armed with a long pole with a hook on the end, had just tried to drag me overboard.

"Clear off!" Tod screamed, hitting him with an oar. "Get out of here!"

The boat rocked again and something fell in the water.

"Kid!" yelled the Blonde. "Kid! They've got him! They've got him!"

I scanned the dark water but, partly because of the way the boat was rocking, I couldn't see the boy—that is, not until he was pulled up onto one of the barges.

"He's there," I pointed. "They've just pulled him up."

"There's nothing we can do for him," Tod said bluntly. "If we get any closer to the barges, we'll be goners. All of us."

The Blonde was about to dive into the water, but I stopped her. "You'll never make it with that leg," I said.

She shook me off angrily. "Well, I'm not leaving my brother to them!"

"I'll go," I said quickly.

"Are you crazy?" Nucky cried.

"I've been hearing that a little too often lately," I said, pulling off my boots.

"If this is a joke, it's not funny," Tod said, copying me. "But I'm going with you."

"Me too!" Nucky added.

"No, you stay here," I said. "We've always got to have at least one Terror guarding our territory."

I looked at Tod and he nodded. "You distract them; I'll find the kid."

We dived in and swam underwater to the barge where Kid was being held. We cautiously lifted our heads out of the water. The Blonde's brother and two other boys had been tied up and thrown against some sacks.

Hiram, I thought when I recognized him. Why did they take someone as big as him? He can't work the looms. But whatever the factory men had planned for him, I didn't care. I had to think of the Blonde's little brother.

Without needing to speak, Tod understood my plan. He

swam around the barge until he was level with the man steering it. Before the man had any idea what was happening, he grabbed him by the legs and pulled him into the water.

"What the . . . ?" one of the other two men on board exclaimed.

I hoisted myself up onto the barge, surprising him from behind, and grabbed the abandoned pole with the hook. "Take this!" I cried, hitting him across the head. The man slumped over in a daze, and I pushed him into the river.

"Listen, brat, maybe you don't know who you're—" the last man on board started saying. I swung the pole at him. He jumped back and dodged it, but lost his balance and fell into the water as well.

Meanwhile, Tod was wrestling with the other two men. It was two to one, but Tod had grown up by the river. No one swims faster than a mud lark, and Tod was wearing them out.

"Tod!" I yelled. "I'm coming!" I bent down over Kid and untied the ropes from his wrists. "Swim as fast as you can to the wharf and then hide underneath it. Do you understand?"

He nodded in fear but jumped into the water. I freed the second Scabby Dog and then looked at Hiram. The circus boy was glaring at me. He would have preferred to stay there, tied up and helpless, rather than let me save him. And, for a moment, I was tempted to leave him there. But it wouldn't have been worthy of what Old Sal had taught me. So I bent down and untied the ropes. By way of thanks, Hiram jumped to his feet, gave me a good shove, and, without a word, jumped into the water.

"Idiot," I muttered.

Just then, Tod climbed back onto the barge. "You rescued them all?"

I nodded. "And the factory men?"

Tod pointed to a distant barge. "They got on that one. Now let's get out of here before they decide to come back."

He didn't have to tell me twice. We swam ashore and hid under the fisherman's wharf, where we found Nucky, the Blonde, and her brother. "I owe you one, Clay," she said when she saw me.

"I was the one who owed you," I answered. "Now we're even."

"The only one who's come out of this badly is me!" exclaimed Tod, dabbing a bloody eyebrow.

We burst out laughing and stayed hidden there until the first light of dawn. Once we were sure the danger had passed, we headed home.

EIGHT

The next morning, all of London—the London of the mud larks, at least—knew every detail about what I'd done. As the hours went by, people's admiration for me, as well as completely ridiculous details, grew.

"Hey, Clay," Tod said, coming back from a swim in the river. "I hear you saved a dozen kids from the factory men last night. And do you want to know what you did it with?"

"Let's hear it," I answered, as I sat on the ground with Nucky, sorting the sellable items from the ones too damaged by the water to be worth anything.

"A pistol and a musket."

"Nothing more unlikely," I said with a laugh. "Though Old Sal probably has a musket hidden somewhere."

"That's what people say." Tod grinned. "And someone swears they even heard you shout, 'God save the queen!' as you were climbing onto the barge. Of course, no one's talking about me. You did it all by yourself. How unfair."

Nucky was laughing so much he was having convulsions. Tod and I joined in, and, for a moment, everything seemed perfect. Mist had finally accepted me, I'd saved some helpless kids from being chained up to looms, and, amazingly, Nucky and Tod were arguing less than usual.

"Hey, isn't that your girlfriend?" Tod suddenly asked, pointing in the direction of the fisherman's wharf.

I turned to see Ollie stumbling through the mud toward us. I stood up. "Ollie!" I called out and went to meet her. "What are you doing here? What's happened?"

Ollie paused to catch her breath. "It's Mist," she gasped, doubling over. "He's disappeared."

"Mist?" Nucky and Tod had heard and were now looking at me questioningly. "Who is Mist?" Tod wanted to know.

"I don't have time to explain," I cut him off. "Ollie, what do you mean 'disappeared'?"

"That this morning the cage had disappeared from the menagerie," she answered.

"The cage? The whole cage has disappeared?"

"Yes. Parson and Hiram say they don't know a thing, but . . ." Ollie gazed across the river, which glowed leaden under the cloud-covered sky. "Clay, I think that Hiram . . ."

"No!" I cried, horrified by the idea. "No, no! He can't have!"

"Hiram? That idiot from last night?" asked Tod.

"I don't have time, Tod!" I snapped.

"What are you so mad about, Clay?" Nucky asked. "We only want to know what's going on."

"You can't!"

"What do you mean?" Tod said with an air of disappointment as he put his hand on my shoulder.

"Tod, leave me alone," I told him. My head was spinning and my face was hot. Hiram couldn't have done it. He couldn't have dumped Mist's cage in the river to get revenge on me. Mist couldn't be dead. Not like that. Not locked in a cage with no chance of escaping. With no chance to fight for his life. With no dignity.

"I said leave me alone!" I yelled when I felt Tod's hand on my shoulder again. *"Leave me alone, Tod!"* I yelled once more, pushing him away.

"Clay, have you gone mad?" Nucky said, stepping between Tod and me. "You don't even look like you."

"You don't understand!" I exclaimed.

Mist was dead. I started running. I ran across Blackfriars Bridge, dived into the laneways behind St. Paul's, dodging wagons and carriages, then headed west without stopping to breathe.

No, no, was the only thing I could think. No.

I ran and ran, and when I finally collapsed exhausted at the foot of Westminster Bridge, I was forced to admit that no matter how far I ran, I'd never be able to escape from myself and the terrible knowledge that I'd have with me for the rest of my life: Hiram hadn't really killed Mist. I had.

"What did I tell you? A fat dog, that's what those circus charlatans wanted to show us. You can't trust rogues like that."

"I'm not surprised they're leaving. I bet they'll never set foot in London again."

"You mark my words, they never had a wolf. They made the whole thing up to sell a few more tickets."

"Too bad half the city now wants their money back! They're ruined!"

From the dock workers to the beggars of St. Paul's, from the seamstresses to the starched-collared nannies, all the residents of the capital had been talking about just one thing for the last week: the sudden and inexplicable disappearance of the main attraction at Smith & Sparrow's Amazing Circus, the Wild Beast of the North.

It had all happened in the space of a night. A brushstroke of black paint had removed the wolf from all the posters around the city. London had woken up and had found itself a new scandal to speculate on.

"So, young man, are we going to do this deal or not?"

Madame Lorna's commanding voice brought me back to reality. I stopped listening to the conversations around me and turned my attention back to the woman who was looking at me perplexedly from across the counter.

"Sorry," I muttered, pulling the merchandise out from my pocket: four bronze pins. "Here they are."

"Not bad," Madame Lorna said, pouring herself her usual shot of Pimm's. "How much do you want?"

I shrugged. "How much have you got?"

Madame Lorna burst out laughing. "You're really not cut out for doing business. Why didn't you send the other one here? The stunted one? He knows how to fool his customers."

Because he hasn't spoken to me for a week, I thought. Tod either.

"Nucky's busy," I answered. "Will we call it a florin?"

Madame Lorna took the money out from a pocket inside the sleeve of her dress. "Well, if you say so."

I took the money and thanked the woman with a nod. Before I could turn to go, she squeezed my wrist. I looked up. "Are you all right, lad?"

I nodded. "Yes."

"You're a bad businessman and a bad liar."

I smiled apologetically. "I never said I was perfect."

Madame Lorna let me go. She seemed to be about to say something else, but her attention was drawn to the bell over the pub door and the arrival of her poor husband. Any concern she had for me vanished. "Alfie, where have you been? I've been waiting for you for hours, you good-for-nothing!"

I let Madame Lorna concentrate on harassing her husband and left the tavern to wander aimlessly. I knew that sooner or later I'd have to make peace with Tod and Nucky—after all, I was still one of the Terrors of Blackfriars Bridge. But the truth was that I didn't want to see the river. I didn't want to smell it or hear it. I didn't want to think that Mist was on the bottom somewhere, now food for the fish. Even if I tried to explain to Tod and Nucky how I felt, I knew they wouldn't understand. Old Sal, on the other hand, would have understood perfectly. But the last thing I needed was for someone to force me to look into my soul. I mean, I was doing fine alone. At least, that's what I kept telling myself.

A few days later, I was wandering in no particular direction along Bayswater Road, a wide, tree-lined street that runs along the north side of Hyde Park. It was an area I never went to, but since fighting with Tod and Nucky, I had a lot of free time on my hands.

"Evening edition!" a boy near the Italian Gardens was yelling, with a stack of newspapers under his arm. "Evening edition! Hey, you there, do you believe in ghosts?" he asked, waving a newspaper under my nose.

"Unfortunately for you, no," I answered without stopping.

"Evening edition! Bloodthirsty ghost on the loose in Smithfield Market! Four cows and five pigs devoured! Evening edition!"

I turned around and grabbed the newspaper from the boy. "You'll have to pay for that!" he protested.

I rummaged through my trouser pockets and gave him a coin. "Where is it?" I asked, searching through the pages. It was one of those illustrated newspapers with more pictures than words. "Where's the article about the ghost at the market?"

"How should I know," he answered. "I can't read. Evening edition!"

Cursing, I leaned up against the park fence and frantically searched for the article. "Here it is," I muttered. There was no mistaking it. Under the sensational title "Bloodthirsty Ghost Terrorizes Butchers!" an illustrator with a taste for the macabre had drawn a creature halfway between a human and an animal devouring a cow in a pool of blood.

I started reading.

On the night of July 25, several Smithfield butchers claim to have seen a creature of uncertain appearance prowling the area. The being, which according to witnesses moves at supernatural speed, devoured numerous beasts, leaving the carcasses as evidence of its insatiable hunger.

"A creature of uncertain appearance that moves at supernatural speed," I muttered to myself. I quickly closed the newspaper. For the first time in days, I was brave enough to look toward the river.

Mist was alive.

It was amazing how efficiently a circus the size of Smith

& Sparrow had packed itself up into an orderly caravan of wagons so quickly. By the time I got to the clearing in Westminster, there was almost nothing left of the circus. Everything had been taken apart and packed away, and the only signs that the big tent had ever been there were the holes in the ground where the poles had been.

Now that there was as good as nothing left to watch, the watchmen on horseback were gone, too, so I didn't bother trying to go unnoticed when I climbed over the wooden fence. And everyone else was too busy with the final packing to pay any attention to me.

I saw Ollie with her grandmother and other fortune tellers, but I kept going straight ahead. I'd say hello to her later. There was someone else I had to talk to first.

I found Hiram polishing some saddles. He was alone, sitting on a crate behind one of the animal wagons. I stood with both legs planted firmly on the ground in front of him, but he kept on polishing the saddles without looking up.

"You didn't do it, did you?"

Hiram finished polishing a saddle and threw it onto a pile, then picked up another muddy one and began cleaning it.

"Do what?"

"You didn't dump Mist's cage in the river."

Hiram smiled grimly. "Mist. What an idiotic name."

"Answer me."

"Why should I?"

"Because you owe me your life."

"I don't owe you anything!" Hiram growled, red in the face as he stood up, clenching his fists.

I grabbed him by the collar and pushed him up against the cage behind him. The bear cage. "I can play this game, too, Hiram."

The bear, who'd been lurking at the back of the wagon a moment before, came up to the bars.

"Let me go! Are you crazy?" Hiram cried.

He was bigger than me, even bigger than Tod. He could have easily gotten free. But there he was, paralyzed by fear, paralyzed by the same violence he'd inflicted on others all his life.

"Tell me what you did with Mist. Actually, what you and your gang did with him. Because I'm sure you didn't do it by yourself. You don't have the guts."

The bear brought its nose up to Hiram's head and started sniffing it. Hiram turned white. "W-we . . . we . . ."

"You?"

"We took him to the forest!" he exclaimed, closing his eyes as the bear continued to sniff him.

"Be more specific. Which forest?"

"The one south of the river," Hiram answered. "Past the big abandoned tannery."

"And what did you do there?"

"We . . . we dropped the cage into a pit. I thought the wolf wouldn't be able to get free and it'd just die of hunger."

I pushed an elbow into Hiram's throat. "Ugly, cruel, disgusting . . ."

For a moment, my mind filled with the worst kind of thoughts. I imagined tying Hiram to the bars of the bear's cage and letting the animal take its revenge. I dreamed of locking him in the lions' cage or the pigs' cage, since they'd even get rid of his bones. Then I came to my senses. I thought about the man with the blue tattoos and our one short conversation.

"You're not like Hiram."

"I know."

"Then don't behave like him."

He was right. I wasn't like Hiram. I was better than him. Hurting him wouldn't make me feel any better. Well . . . it might a little, but not really.

I let him go, and he instantly sprang away from the bear cage. "This d-doesn't end here!" he gasped, as pale as a ghost. "Do you hear me, river boy? This doesn't end here!"

"No, Hiram. It's over now," I answered. "And I'll give you

some advice: try living your life without having to ruin the lives of others. You might even like it."

Hiram didn't answer but, from the way he looked at me, I knew he'd never stop hurting others. In that moment, I felt a deep pain for that boy who was unable to give love because he'd probably never received any.

NINE

The only hope I had of finding Mist was to join one of the many hunting parties that had formed around the city as word spread that the Wild Beast of the North was alive and on the loose.

"That villain!" Ollie exclaimed when, after my fight with Hiram, I told her what I'd discovered. "Smith and Sparrow have been treating the animal keepers very badly for days. They even fired two of them after accusing them of being responsible for the wolf's disappearance!"

She went straight to Smith and Sparrow to tell them the truth. Hiram was immediately summoned and they, together with Parson, pressed him until he confessed.

The two owners then published an advertisement in every newspaper in the city, offering a big reward to anyone who brought the animal back to the menagerie. But, as I soon discovered, there were more hunters who wanted to kill Mist and display his skin over their fireplace as a trophy than hunters who wanted the reward money.

When I went by to see Old Sal, there was no need to explain anything to him. Like always.

"Sal, I've got to find him," I said. "I've got to stop them from killing him."

"I certainly won't stand in your way," he answered from his armchair as he leafed through an old Bible.

"I'm going to have to join one of those hunting parties."

"No," Old Sal replied. "You mustn't join just any party. You're going to need to be guided by the most skilled and ruthless hunter of all. The hunter who'd do anything to kill Britain's last living wolf."

"Who is it? Do you know him?"

Sal nodded. "His name is Stephen Brackenbury. You'll find him at Madame Lorna's tavern."

I didn't know how to thank Old Sal. From the day he adopted me, he'd always supported me in every decision I made.

He took his pipe from his mouth and looked at me with his bright blue eyes. "Good luck, lad."

I walked over and hugged him. Perhaps the only way to thank him was to find Mist, save him, and come home again. First, though, I had to get this Brackenbury to take me with him. At any cost.

I got to Madame Lorna's tavern around dinnertime. The place was crowded, and there was a strange electricity in the air—the same one that you felt in the city before a big event. And the wolf hunt was a big event.

"He'll get it," I heard a man say as I stepped inside. "No doubt about it."

"Aye," his friend agreed. "Brackenbury uses his rifle as if it were a part of him."

Madame Lorna was surveying her realm from behind the counter with a frown, while her husband busied himself with serving the crowd of customers. I went straight over to her. If there was anyone who could help me, it was her.

"Clay, what are you doing here? Do you have some business for me?"

"No," I answered. "I want to hunt the wolf."

"Bad idea."

"With Brackenbury," I added.

Madame Lorna looked at me in surprise. "I thought you were the brightest one of your trio, Clay."

I shrugged. "I've decided to change my life."

The woman raised an eyebrow and put her hands on her hips. "And what does Old Sal think of you changing your life?"

"He was the one who sent me here."

Somehow, that seemed to fix things. Madame Lorna left the counter and gestured to me to follow her. As she passed, the patrons stepped aside, partly out of respect, partly because of her imposing size.

She led me to the back of the room where, sitting at an old rectangular table, was Brackenbury himself, surrounded by half a dozen big, beefy men. Except for one, that is: a young man in his twenties with a horseface and buck teeth.

Brackenbury wasn't the biggest man at the table, but he didn't need to be. His face and expression more than made up for his lack of bulk. They showed a harshness and a lack of compassion that I'd never seen before in my life, even among the most ruthless mud larks.

I saw at once that Brackenbury was a born killer. It was part of him.

"Brackenbury," Madame Lorna said, and the men at the table instantly stopped talking. "There's someone here who wants to meet you."

The hunter's dark eyes turned to me. "What for?"

Madame Lorna put a hand on my shoulder. "I think the boy might be a good addition to your hunting party."

The horse-faced man burst out laughing. "Who? This one?"

"Sly," Brackenbury growled at him, "shut up." The hunter looked at Madame Lorna, waiting for the rest of the story.

"He's nimble and fast," she said. "And strong. He's used to digging in the mud for hours."

Brackenbury didn't seem particularly impressed. "Sly can ride for a whole day without even stopping to piss."

"He's Old Sal's adopted son," Madame Lorna added. "He's the one who sent him."

The hunter finally looked surprised. For an instant—but just an instant—his eyes softened. "Good Old Sal," he muttered. "We fought together in Crimea centuries ago." He stared at me. "I hope you know how worthy the man is who raised you. If I take you on, I'll only be doing it for him. I owe my life to that devil."

I had no idea that Sal had fought in Crimea. I had no idea where Crimea even was, to be honest. There were so many things I didn't know about Sal. I didn't know where he was born, if he'd always lived in London, or if he'd had a different life before he was a mud lark. I'd only ever taken from Old Sal.

I made a promise to myself that when I saw him again, I'd ask him all those questions I hadn't asked in all these years.

Brackenbury slapped his hand on the table. "I'll take you. An extra pair of eyes will come in handy. But there's a condition: you have to do exactly what I tell you. Understand, boy?"

"Yes, sir," I replied.

"Two days' time, dawn, out the front of Smithfield Market. We'll start there."

When Madame Lorna walked me to the front door, she had a grim look. "I hope you know what you're doing, lad," she said. "And I hope that you really want to kill the wolf. Because, if not . . . God help you."

The next morning, I found Tod and Nucky at work as usual, busily filling a large wicker basket with the things they'd pulled out from the mud. Tod saw me first, but he quickly looked away, frowning and continuing to throw things into the basket. Nucky, though, smiled.

"Hello, lads," I said, stopping a few steps away, my hands buried in my trouser pockets. Why did apologizing have to be so hard?

"Hello, Clay," Nucky replied. "Are you all right?"

I nodded and looked at Tod. I knew it wasn't going to be easy with him. "Hello, Tod."

He didn't answer.

Nucky tried to lighten the mood. "We've found a lot of interesting stuff. Even a whole tea set in a box. Some thief must have wanted to get rid of the stolen goods as fast as possible!" He chuckled.

"Lucky," I said.

Come on, Tod, look at me, I thought to myself. Please.

Tod continued to throw things into the basket in silence. Nucky scratched his head as if he was embarrassed and tried to help me again. I didn't deserve it.

"You'll never guess what Tod found this morning. A ring! It's lost its gem but the setting is gold. If I get a good price, we'll have food for at least a month."

"Not bad," I said, trying to sound cheerful. "You seem to be doing well without me."

Tod stopped working and jumped to his feet. Without a word, he turned and started striding away.

Nucky looked at me. "If I were you, I'd go talk to him. He didn't take the wolf thing well."

"What about you, Nucky? How did you take it?"

Nucky shrugged. "You lied to us, Clay. You've never done that before. Maybe you had your reasons. Or maybe you thought you did. But now shake a leg and go talk to Tod. You know what he's like."

Tod had stopped a hundred yards away and was staring at the river with a frown. I joined him and stood silently by his side, waiting for the right moment to speak.

Tod suddenly turned to me. "Clay, how could you keep something like that from us? Did you think we wouldn't understand? Are we too stupid for you?"

"The opposite," I answered calmly. "I was sure you'd think it was crazy."

"Because it is crazy! But do you know what? If my brother—my brother, Clay—makes a decision, no matter how crazy it might be, I take his side. Always." Tod shook his head. "What an idiot I am."

I'd never felt so in the wrong in my life. I was no saint and I'd been wrong in the past, but not with Tod and Nucky. I'd never let them down, and it was a horrible feeling.

Tod threw his hands in the air. "You've got nothing to say?"

"I don't know what to say," I admitted. "Except that you're right and I'm sorry."

We both stood there in silence looking at the river, while all around us, the lives of others, unaware of our drama, flowed by like always. Mud larks digging in the mud. Toshers headed for the sewers. Dock laborers carrying crates and barrels.

"So what's your plan now?" Tod sighed.

I looked at him without understanding. "What do you mean?"

"The wolf. Even if I can't read, I've got good ears. Half the city is going to hunt him down."

"I'm part of that half. Thanks to Sal and Madame Lorna, I've joined a hunting party. We start tomorrow morning."

Tod nodded. "It won't be easy for the two of us to protect our territory alone. The Tower Hounds are upping their game, but Nucky and I will manage. You go save your wolf. It's the least you can do, after all the mess you've made."

Tod walked toward the bridge. As he passed me, I stopped him by putting a hand on his shoulder. "Tod."

"Aye?"

"Thank you." I looked him in the eye. "Seriously."

"Just make it back in one piece. I can't even imagine spending the rest of my life alone with Nucky. I'd end up killing him."

"I'll try."

"You'd better."

Then Tod walked away. I watched him follow the riverbank, until he finally disappeared behind the fisherman's wharf.

TEN

That night, I went back to the circus for the last time.

The mood was grim. No bonfires, no drinking and performing, no patrols of watchmen on horseback. I climbed over the fence and walked with my head bowed toward where the fortune tellers were. Ollie had told me that the wagon she shared with her grandmother was painted with the colors of the old didicoy's homeland. It was easy to find. Its big wooden wheels were painted a beautiful bright red, the main body was canary yellow, while the shutters and the roof were bright blue. A majestic black eagle was painted over the door, but I had no idea what it meant.

I knocked. After a few moments, the door opened. "Good

evening," I said, hastily removing my tattered hat. "I'm looking for Ollie, please. Is she here?"

Her grandmother narrowed her dark eyes to focus on me better. Up close, she was even older than I'd thought, her tanned face lined with wrinkles that looked like they'd been carved with a knife, while her hair was a strange bluish white.

"1788," she said in English but with a heavy accent.

"Pardon?"

"I was born in 1788," she explained. "You were wondering how old I am."

"Oh," I muttered in surprise. "But how did you . . . ?"

"I don't need cards to read people," she said. "Especially transparent ones like you. It's like looking through a waterfall."

I didn't know what to say, so I remained silent, standing there at the door. I was beginning to understand why Hiram was afraid of the didicoy and thought she was a witch.

"Oh, for goodness sake!" she muttered.

I jumped. "I didn't mean that I—"

"I know," she cut me off. "My granddaughter is over there."

I turned but saw nothing for a moment. I was about to ask the old woman to explain how she'd read my mind, when Ollie emerged from behind a dark wagon, holding a bucket of water.

I went over to her. "Hello."

"Hello," she said guardedly, putting the bucket down.

"I just met your grandmother," I said. "I don't think she likes me."

Ollie raised an eyebrow. "If she didn't like you, you wouldn't be here, believe me." She rubbed her hands. "So why are you here?"

"I'm leaving in the morning," I explained. "I'm going to find Mist."

"I've seen some men trying to catch him. They look like a bad lot."

"And I'm going with the worst of them."

Ollie's eyes lit up with a light I'd never seen before. Admiration. "I've underestimated you, river boy."

I held out my hand, and she shook it. "Thank you for your help. Without you, I never would have met Mist."

"And you think that would have been a bad thing?"

"I don't think it," I said. "I know it."

"So have a nice trip."

Ollie picked up the bucket and continued walking to the wagon. Just before she stepped inside, she turned. I saw her playing with the bracelets that jangled on her wrists. She came back toward me and, without a word, thrust something into my hand. Then she disappeared into the wagon.

When I opened my hand, I saw a golden coin-shaped pendant. A good luck charm. I needed it badly. I squeezed it in my fist and slipped it into my pocket.

In silence, I left the circus, sure I'd never see her again.

Protecting Mist wasn't going to be easy. That became obvious the moment I got to Smithfield Market the next morning and saw Brackenbury on a splendid dark horse holding his rifle with a menacing look. His party was behind him, including the young man with the buck teeth. As soon as he saw me, he gave me a nasty look and spat on the ground.

"So here's Old Sal's adopted son," said Brackenbury. "You can ride, can't you, boy?"

I'd only been on a horse once in my life, when Old Sal had taken me to see some friends of his in the country. But I was tiny at the time. There was no reason to tell the hunter that, though, so I nodded confidently. After all, all I had to do was stay in the saddle. "Of course."

"Good." He nodded. "Sly," he called.

The young man stepped forward, leading a brown horse that was a little smaller than the others by the reins. "Here, mud lark."

The way he said the last word left no doubt: Sly despised everything I was and stood for. I took the reins, forcing a smile. I couldn't afford to have enemies in the party. They all had to believe that I really wanted to kill Mist. "Thank you."

Sly didn't answer but went back to his own horse, immediately turning his back on me.

"All right, folks," Brackenbury began. "The first stop is Romford Farm in Seven Kings. It's the last place the wolf was seen." We'll track him from there."

⁂

The Romfords were quite an old couple with a chicken farm. It was small and rundown, with one part surrounded by a low stone wall, and a vegetable garden and a chicken coop around the back.

"I went out after dinner as usual last night to lock up the chickens," said Mr. Romford. "We had a fox around here a few weeks ago, so, to avoid any surprises, I started locking up the chickens every night. But this morning, when I went to let them out . . ." The farmer shook his head. "You've seen what it did, haven't you? All of them! It killed all of them! It didn't even leave one alive!"

Brackenbury, who'd listened to the farmer's tale with an expression devoid of compassion, dismounted and began to carefully search the ground around the farm, followed by his men.

"What are they doing?" Romford asked me. I had no idea, but luckily Sly answered.

"We're looking for tracks. Not just from its paws, but also its scent. He definitely would have left his scent somewhere to mark the territory, even if he was just passing through."

"So you don't think he'll come back?" asked Romford hopefully.

Sly shook his head. "He'll head north. Back where he came from." Then he looked at me. "If you're done resting, mud lark, there's work to be done."

I ignored his gibe and got off my horse to start searching behind the farmhouse. I had absolutely no experience doing this kind of thing, but I was hoping for a stroke of luck. If I could find Mist's tracks first, I could cover them.

"There's something here!" Sly suddenly yelled, motioning to the others to come over. Brackenbury and the rest of the party were quickly there.

"What, boy? What?" asked the hunter, his eyes shining.

"Tracks," Sly declared proudly. "Here. As clear as day."

Brackenbury slapped him on the back. "Well done, my boy, well done."

Hearing those words, Sly's horseface filled with pride.

"We follow them," Brackenbury ordered. "But take it easy: the wolf moves at night and hides during the day. We'll have a better chance of catching it when it's dark. So when the sun goes down, the real hunt begins."

"Understand, mud lark?" Sly hissed as he passed me. "Be ready. The hunt's about to begin."

"Halt!"

We were riding along a narrow path that followed the River Great Ouse, near the village of Hartford, when Brackenbury lifted a hand, motioning for us to stop.

For the past seven days, I'd been pretending to be enthusiastic about hunting Mist and going down in history as one of the men who killed Britain's last living wolf. And I must have been pretty convincing, because neither Brackenbury nor his men seemed to have the slightest suspicion of me.

It was a different story with Sly, though. Every time I looked over my shoulder, I found his suspicious eyes on my back. Whenever I opened my mouth to say something (and it didn't happen often, since I didn't have much to say), he never missed an opportunity to challenge or question me.

"Why should a mud lark want to hunt a wolf?" he'd asked me on the first day, as we were leaving the Romfords' farm. "You can't shoot and you ride like a girl."

"I got tired of digging in the mud," I answered. "As for the other stuff," I added, looking at Sly's rifle, "I can always learn."

"Sure, of course." He laughed before spurring on his horse and leaving me behind.

"There are two big farms about ten miles from here," Brackenbury explained when we were all gathered around him. "The first follows the course of the river. The second one is located along the road to Alconbury. Both have cattle. The wolf might have decided to pay a visit to one of them. I need two volunteers to go exploring."

"Me!" I immediately cried.

"Good. You go to the farm in Alconbury," Brackenbury said. "Who else?"

Glaring at me, Sly put up his hand. "I can do both. I ride fast, I do."

"No," Brackenbury answered. "It would still take too long. We camp here. Both of you be quick." Looking disappointed, Sly dug his heels into his horse and disappeared in a cloud of dust. My departure was much less impressive, but as soon as I was out of sight of the hunters, I did my best to encourage my horse. I wanted to get to Alconbury as soon as possible to find out if Mist had been seen there. And if he had, I was going to keep the news to myself and throw Brackenbury off the scent.

When I got to the farm near Alconbury, I immediately knew that Mist had been there. Half a dozen men with rifles were standing menacingly around the farmhouse. There were no women or children to be seen, much less animals, which must have all been locked up in the barns and chicken coops.

Damn, I thought as I approached the fence.

"Good morning," I said to the eldest of the group, a man with a tanned face and white hair.

The man raised his hand in greeting. "Good morning to you, young man. You're not from around here, are you?"

"No, sir," I answered. "My hunting party is on the trail of the wolf that escaped from the circus in London. Has he been here?"

"He sure has!" one of the younger boys exclaimed, unable to hold back his excitement. "And just last night! I was taking the pigs back to their pen when there he was right in front of me, a two-hundred-pound, yellow-eyed monster! I was all ready to meet my maker, and then my grandfather came out of the house shooting and that rascal ran away!"

"Did you wound him?" I immediately asked the old man, trying to hide my concern. If Mist had been wounded, he'd certainly be leaving a trail of blood behind him, which Brackenbury wouldn't take long to find.

"Not even close," the man answered. "It disappeared into the trees as fast as the wind. The idea that a beast like that is out there, free and uncontrolled . . ." He looked toward the house. "I've got seven grandchildren, the youngest is just a year old. They haven't been out of the house all day, and, as far as I'm concerned, they'll stay locked up in there until that devil has met the fate he deserves: nailed to a wall."

That devil wouldn't even be here if he hadn't been captured and locked in a cage, I thought to myself angrily. He'd be miles away, hidden in the forests of the north and living his life without bothering anyone.

"Thank you for your help," I said, turning my horse.

"You're welcome, young man. I hope you kill the beast."

By the time I reached the hunting party, Sly was back from his expedition and was talking to Brackenbury.

". . . they haven't seen him over there," I heard him say. "I even asked in the nearby villages."

Brackenbury nodded grimly, then saw me. "What news

do you have?" he asked hopefully. "Did the wolf go through Alconbury?"

"No," I answered firmly. "No sightings."

"Are you sure?" Sly immediately asked suspiciously.

"Why would I lie?" I snapped.

"I don't know," he answered. "You tell me."

"If you like, we can go back there together and talk to the farmer again."

Sly seemed to be waiting for nothing else. "Excellent. Let's go."

"No one's going anywhere," Brackenbury growled. "We don't have time to waste. Especially now that we've lost the tracks. Tonight, we'll split up into two teams. You two," he said, glaring at Sly and me, "you'll both stay with me, so you can stop squabbling like sulky little girls. Now, eat something and get some rest. It's going to be a long night."

And from the look Sly gave me, I knew it really would be.

It had never been as clear to me as it was that night how much I was a river boy through and through. From the way the Thames was flowing, I could tell if it would rise or fall the next day. From the color of the water, I could work out if it had rained in Kemble, the remote village in

Gloucestershire where the Thames started. I was able to swim in total darkness and, from the way the waves hit the pillars of the bridge, tell what kind of boat was going past.

What I wasn't used to doing, though, was walking in a forest, in the dark and without a single point of reference, looking for tracks I couldn't see.

"Mud lark, would you stop making so much noise? Even a deaf and blind boar would notice you. Why the hell Brackenbury brought you with us is a mystery."

Believe me, friend, I wonder that, too, I thought as I continued following Sly through the trees, trying to put my feet where he'd put his. Brackenbury was ahead of us with two hunters called Thorpe and Reeves. Thorpe, who was a particularly good tracker, bent down from time to time to check the ground.

"There's something here," he suddenly announced.

We all stopped. My hands went cold. "Is it the wolf?" I asked, unable to keep quiet.

Thorpe kneeled and examined the tracks in the moonlight.

"This time it's not going to get away," Sly muttered, stroking the barrel of his rifle. "We're going to get that bastard."

I clenched my fists, hiding them in my pockets, as I stared at Thorpe, waiting for him to deliver his verdict.

"The shape's right," he finally decided. "Narrow, elongated, middle toes forward, but . . ."

"But?" asked Sly.

But? I thought.

"It's too small to be our wolf's," Thorpe concluded. "It must be a fox."

I closed my eyes and silently gave thanks to heaven. When I opened them, Sly was staring at me.

"You look relieved, mud lark," he said.

"Anything but," I answered, immediately turning my back on him and setting off after the others.

We continued silently for almost an hour, stopping occasionally when Thorpe thought he'd found a track.

"Stop," he said for the umpteenth time, before bending down again to inspect the ground.

"Give me some good news, Thorpe, damn it," Brackenbury swore, leaning back against a tree. "That hellish beast is around here somewhere. I can feel it."

Thorpe nodded. "Yes."

"Yes?" I asked. "Yes what?"

"Calm down, mud lark." Brackenbury laughed. "You're almost more eager than me to kill this animal!"

Sly muttered something under his breath, but I ignored him.

"So, Thorpe? Are you going to say something? We're not in some damned theater! Don't keep us in suspense!" growled Brackenbury, bending down near Thorpe.

"It's him," Thorpe confirmed. "It's our wolf. And that's not all."

Brackenbury's eyes shone with a hunger. "What are you talking about?"

"The tracks are fresh. It just passed through here."

Sly looked around, lifting his rifle. "Come on, you bastard. Show yourself," he murmured.

I started sweating. Run, Mist, run, I wished.

Without taking his eyes off the ground, Thorpe began following Mist's tracks. All four of us came after him. Brackenbury, Reeves, and Sly all hoping to spot the wolf. Me, on the other hand, praying that Mist was as far away from there as possible.

"Damn it, mud lark, you almost seem to be making noises on purpose!" Sly snapped when I stepped on a branch.

"Shut up back there!" Brackenbury growled. "You'll panic him. Not another word out of either of you!"

We covered a long distance through the forest, straining our eyes and ears for some sign. Suddenly, Thorpe pointed south and began moving downhill.

Water, I guessed after a few minutes. I could smell it. For

a moment, knowing something that the others didn't made me feel better. Shortly after, though, when a large body of water opened before us, my heart almost stopped.

An animal was drinking.

An animal that could have been Mist.

Brackenbury raised his hand and we all stopped. He then looked at me, making me understand that I had to stay where I was since I was the only one without a weapon. The moment Brackenbury started moving, Thorpe, Reeves, and Sly each began walking in a different direction. They were going to surround him.

I waited for them to get far enough away and then, in a panic, sprinted toward the lake, praying I wouldn't run into any of the hunters in the dark. I reached the shore, took off my boots, and slipped into the water as silently as only a mud lark can. I went completely underwater and swam in the direction of the animal, which was still standing on the other side of the lake, unaware of anything.

Then, just as I was about to come up for air, I heard a shot.

And a long howl of pain.

ELEVEN

I brought my head up out of the water, gasping for air, and immediately looked toward the bank. Mist was gone, and I could hear Brackenbury's angry cries.

They didn't catch him! I thought, feeling relieved. They didn't catch him!

"Mist!" I called quietly. "Mist!"

But the wolf was gone. I went quickly back to get my boots and tried to find one of the others. Unfortunately, though, I ran into Sly.

"Did you take a swim, mud lark?" he said angrily.

"Where's the wolf? Did you shoot him?"

"Do you really care or are you just here to enjoy the show?"

Sly answered with a shove.

"Answer me! Did you shoot him?" I exclaimed in exasperation. I was on the verge of giving myself away, but my concern for Mist was getting the better of me.

"You answer me first: what the hell is a mud lark doing here, in the middle of a forest, chasing a damned wolf?"

"I already told you!" I cried.

Realizing that Sly wasn't going to tell me anything, I started walking away, but he stopped me. "You'll have to make an effort and tell me again, then."

For a moment, an image of Mist filled my mind. I saw him lying on the ground, bleeding, at the mercy of Brackenbury, who was getting ready to skin him.

"I don't have to do anything!" I yelled, grabbing Sly by the collar. "Nothing!"

"Get your hands off me, mud lark!" he screamed, putting a hand on his rifle. "Or I swear—"

"What are you two doing?" Brackenbury's voice surprised us from behind. "Stop wasting time! Thorpe has found traces of blood!" He looked at Sly. "You finally did something good, boy, even though you should have waited for my signal before shooting. Now let's get moving. The wolf isn't far away."

Not knowing what else to do, I let Sly go. Mist was injured.

How serious was it? And if we found him, defenseless and bleeding, how would I defend him against four armed hunters?

Brackenbury led Sly and me to where the trail of blood began. Thorpe was bending over, looking at the ground. "Well?" Brackenbury demanded. "Which way did he go?"

"This animal is smart," Thorpe said. "You see all these broken, bloodstained branches? It went in circles for a while, before deciding what direction to take."

"So?" asked Brackenbury impatiently.

"So, we should split up," Thorpe suggested.

Hearing his words, I tried not to let my happiness show.

"I'll go with the mud lark," said Sly.

"You don't need to," I answered.

"Have you ever followed a track? No. So I'm going with you," Sly decided.

Brackenbury nodded. "Sly's right. You wouldn't achieve anything by yourself apart from risk getting killed. Come on, everyone, get moving."

I joined Sly, cursing him and his suspicions.

"If you see anything, stop and tell me," he said. "And careful where you put your feet."

I didn't answer but concentrated on the ground and plants, looking for any sign that Mist had been by. I had to be the one to find the tracks so I could erase them. But Sly was as determined as I was.

"Here!" he suddenly exclaimed, pointing at something on the ground with his rifle. "Stop or you'll step on it!"

That was exactly what I'd just tried to do: step on the drop of scarlet blood that was glistening in the moonlight.

Sly stuck two fingers in his mouth and made a strange sound like an owl. After a few minutes, Brackenbury, Thorpe, and Reeves emerged from the undergrowth. *This way*, Sly gestured without speaking.

We set off again, following the drops of blood, which became larger and closer together.

He's losing too much blood, I thought in a panic. He won't be able to outrun us.

Suddenly, Brackenbury put his hand up, turned, and signaled to us to be quiet.

"What—" I began to say, hoping to scare Mist away, but Brackenbury pointed his rifle at me and waved me to shut up.

We'd found the wolf. He was about fifty yards away, sitting and incessantly licking a paw. His fur glowed silver in the moonlight. He was impossible to miss in the dark forest. Brackenbury aimed his rifle. He adjusted his aim a couple of times, then prepared to fire.

In that moment, I realized that we couldn't both survive.

But, Clay, I said to myself, you knew that from the start.

Brackenbury fired.

In the same instant, I screamed, *"Run, Mist! Run!"*

Furious, Brackenbury turned to me and hit me with his rifle butt, knocking me onto the ground as dozens of bright stars exploded before my eyes.

"I knew it!" Sly exclaimed. "I knew he didn't really want to kill the wolf!"

"Where did it go?" I heard Reeves ask.

"Lost in the trees," Thorpe answered. "Damn!"

Brackenbury grabbed me by my collar and brought my face up to his. "So the wolf is your friend, is it?" he hissed. "You've even given it a name. Old Sal shouldn't have done this to me."

"Sal doesn't know anything about it," I quickly said.

"Sal always knows everything," Brackenbury answered. "But before I take care of him, I'll take care of you." He threw me back onto the ground, and immediately everyone had their rifles pointed at me.

"Leave him to me," Sly said. "I suspected him from the start. I even tried warning you, remember?"

After a moment's hesitation, Brackenbury lowered his rifle. The others followed his lead. "Very well. I was wrong about you, Sly. I should have given you more credit.

To you goes the honor of killing this little snake."

Sly held his rifle within inches of my eyes. "Goodbye, mud lark," he hissed. "Finally, I won't have to look at your traitorous face anymore."

So this is the end, I thought. I just hope Brackenbury doesn't really take care of Old Sal when he gets back to London. And Mist . . . With any luck, he'll be able to put enough distance between himself and the hunters.

"I want to give you time to say your prayers, mud lark," Sly said, starting to count. "One. Two. Thr–*Argh!*"

Boom!

The rifle went off a fraction of an inch from my head. I collapsed onto the ground, pressing my hands over my ears. For a few very long moments, I was deaf. So I couldn't hear Sly's screams as Mist sunk his teeth into his arm and forced him to drop the rifle, nor Brackenbury's frantic orders to Thorpe and Reeves in a last desperate attempt to kill the wolf.

Even injured, Mist was too fast for them, and he seemed to know exactly what he was doing. After disarming Sly, instead of finishing him off, he attacked Thorpe and Reeves, sending them running. He left Brackenbury for last. The hunter shot his rifle and missed. He then angrily threw the weapon onto the ground and pulled out the long knife that he wore on his belt. "Go ahead, wolf," he said. "I've killed bigger animals than you with this. You don't scare me."

Mist growled and prepared to attack as I got up off the ground, rubbing my head. Just then, I heard yells from the second team.

"Over here!" Sly yelled back. "We're over here!"

"Mist, let's get out of here!" I said. I picked all the rifles up off the ground, threw them over my shoulder, and started walking away. "Come on!" I urged him, when I saw he was still staring at Brackenbury and baring his fangs. "They're coming to kill you!"

"And we will, boy," hissed the hunter, tossing the knife from one hand to the other like a juggler. "You can count on it."

Lying on the ground with his injured arm, Sly glared at me with hatred. "We'll kill your pet first, then we'll look after you."

Behind me, I could just make out the second team's torches coming closer. "Mist! Let's get out of here!"

After a long moment, Mist turned away from Brackenbury and dived into the trees. I went after him, holding the hunter and Sly at gunpoint.

"We'll meet again soon," Sly threatened.

"I doubt it," I answered.

I desperately hoped we wouldn't.

TWELVE

"Did you hear about the wolf? Apparently there's a big reward for anyone who kills it."

"Kills it? I thought the circus folk wanted it back."

"Not after it attacked a boy. It almost took his arm off."

I was wandering around the market in a small village called Woodford, occasionally picking up some discarded scraps of food off the ground, when I heard this conversation between two women.

Mist and I had been on the run for ten days now, and I could hardly believe that they still hadn't found us. On the night of the fight with Brackenbury, I'd really struggled to keep up with him. And if we'd gone on any longer, I wouldn't have. The wolf ran like the wind through the forest. All I could do was desperately try to keep up, while the voices of the hunters got closer and closer behind me.

Then I'd heard something. Running water.

"Mist," I'd whispered. "This way!" And he'd followed me.

After a few minutes, we'd come to a river and dived straight in so we wouldn't leave any tracks. We'd climbed out again two miles farther south and started running again. Mist had only stopped at the first light of dawn, when he lay down under a tree to rest.

I'd collapsed a few yards from him, exhausted, and thinking about everything that had happened on that long night: the rifle aimed at my face, the shot, Mist appearing from the trees and saving me from the hunters, our escape . . .

It had all really happened. But it wasn't over yet. Half of England was chasing Mist. He'd never be able to reach the north without my help.

"I'll take you home. Do you understand, Mist?" I'd said. "I won't leave you alone."

Now, ten days later, I had almost no strength left. The night marches were getting longer and more exhausting, and the lack of food—proper food—was starting to be a real problem. For a while, I'd been eating acorns and wild apples, but that day, as soon as Mist had stopped to rest and wait for the night, I'd hidden the rifles and walked to the nearest village. Now I was there, though, I wished I'd never set foot in the place.

"Well, I hope they kill him, and quickly, too," said a baker. "My brother has a farm and already has his work cut out for him with foxes. All he'd need is a damned wolf as well!"

Although I didn't believe in stealing, I didn't feel guilty when I slipped a piece of bread into my jacket pocket.

I left the village and followed a long trail before taking refuge in the forest. I found Mist awake, sitting at the foot of a tree. As soon as he saw me, though, he lay down and went back to sleep. I retrieved one of the rifles and hugged it to me. I'd gotten into the habit of sleeping like that, with my back up against a tree and the rifle ready. I was terrified that Brackenbury and his people would catch us asleep and kill Mist right before my eyes.

That evening, the wolf wanted to set out earlier than usual. The sun hadn't set yet, but he was ready to resume our journey.

I got up from the ground in pain, slung the rifles over my shoulder, and started following. I'd learned to always keep a certain distance away, without ever getting too close. When I'd tried to look at his injured leg, he'd growled threateningly, making things clear. Luckily, the leg had healed on its own, even though Mist had limped for a few days.

"You know, Mist, it would be nice if you could talk," I said as we walked through the trees. "At least you'd be company. And then the fact that I always have to keep behind you. . . . Not that your rear end is—"

Snap!

"Oh, God!" I screamed, jumping up and down on one foot. "A trap!"

The toothed jaws had snapped around the heel of my boot but without doing much damage. I bent down to push it back open and free myself.

"Don't move, Mist!" I said, as I carefully scanned the ground. We were crossing a place in the forest with a carpet of low creepers. It was perfect for hiding traps. I picked up a branch and started testing the ground. Mist watched me closely, without moving. "Here's another one," I muttered as the trap snapped shut on the branch. "Damn, we're surrounded." I wasn't wrong. In just a few minutes, I set off four traps, all just a few feet from me.

"I'm coming over there now, Mist," I said, walking cautiously toward him. "Keep still. Just keep—"

"Daddy! Daddy! I've caught a squirrel!"

I stopped in my tracks and turned around, peering

through the trees. Who'd spoken? I realized it was a child when I caught a glimpse of a little blond head through the leaves and branches. I had to get Mist out of there, and fast. But how? The traps were everywhere.

I began to back away slowly, keeping my eyes fixed on the boy, who was too busy examining his catch to notice me. Then something bit into my ankle, piercing my skin, and I fell to the ground with a muffled cry.

The boy jerked his head up and saw me. "Wait!" he said. "You're in one of our traps! I'll let you out."

"No, stay there!" I ordered. "I can do it by myself."

"No, you can't!" protested the boy, pulling a long nail out of his trouser pocket. "See? It only takes a second with this."

He began walking toward me confidently, knowing exactly where to put his feet. When he reached me, he smiled apologetically. "I'm sorry, but everyone around here knows that . . ." His gaze froze on something behind me, he stopped talking with his mouth gaping open in surprise.

"Please don't scream," I pleaded. "He won't hurt you. See? He's good. He's good. He's not like everyone says. Please."

The boy continued to stare at Mist in amazement.

"Nicolas!" I heard a male voice calling. "Nicolas, where have you got to?"

"Please," I pleaded again. "Don't scream or they'll kill him.

The boy looked from Mist to me. "He's yours?" he whispered.

"No," I answered. "He doesn't belong to anyone. And to keep it that way, I need your help. Please."

The boy thought about it for a moment, then nodded. Turning around, he shouted, "I was wrong, Daddy. There was nothing!"

The father said something back that I didn't understand, as the boy bent down and snapped open the trap in an instant. He then stared at Mist again, more amazed than ever. "Look," he said, "I'll show you where the traps are so you don't get hurt." He took my hand and pointed to several places. "There, there, and there. And over there, where that big rock is, and farther down, near that old log. Do you understand?"

I nodded. "Thank you. And thank you from him, too," I said, meaning Mist, who'd stayed motionless the whole time, his amber eyes fixed on the boy. "Don't tell anyone you've seen us, all right? It will be our secret." He nodded. Then, after one last stunned look at Mist, he turned and ran off.

THIRTEEN

Thirty-seven days later, for the first time since our adventure had begun, Mist wanted to set out in the sunlight.

"Mist, I'm tired, let me sleep," I moaned when the wolf started nudging me with his muzzle. "Come on, we've only just stopped."

He'd only been touching me like that for the last few days. For me, though, the rules were still the same: I couldn't get too close to him and, in particular, I wouldn't dare touch him. Mist, on the other hand, came up to me from time to time to smell me, especially when I'd come back from an expedition to some village.

It had been days now, though, since we'd been near where

people lived. I had no idea where we were exactly, but we had to be close to the Scottish border. I'd guessed it from the strange accent the last people I'd spoken to had had and from the colder, windier weather.

Mist gave me a solid blow on the forehead, forcing me to open my eyes. "I'm awake, I'm awake," I muttered. "I'm so hungry," I added, getting to my feet. After over a month of not eating a real meal, I'd become almost as thin as Nucky, if not thinner.

Who knows what he and Tod are doing at the moment, I thought as I walked behind Mist. They're probably lying on the riverbank enjoying the sun. Or they're sitting on the fisherman's wharf counting the money they've made.

I missed them both terribly. I missed listening to them argue. I missed Nucky's revolting stories about the Great Stink of '58 and the disgusted faces Tod would pull, along with the threats he'd make. And I missed Old Sal. I'd never felt such a need for his advice, which always made me think about what's wrong and right, as I had during those weeks.

"Mist, could you slow down a little? We've been walking for hours."

I wasn't sure, but judging from the position of the sun, it must have been mid-afternoon. Mist hadn't stopped since we'd set out. Meanwhile, the landscape around us kept changing, becoming greener and lusher.

Mist kept walking without stopping as I plodded after him, using a cane to help. I still had the rifles I'd stolen from Brackenbury and the other hunters. Even though it was unlikely they'd find us now, I kept carrying them on my shoulder every night, determined to defend Mist to the last.

"Mist, I can't go any farther," I said after nearly a whole day of forced marching. "Mist, let's stop."

And, finally, he did stop.

I looked at him in disbelief. "We're here? Really? This is your home?"

It had to be. All around, I saw nothing but hills covered with emerald grass and, in the distance in front of us, the dark patch of a forest. It was remote and wild, the perfect hiding place.

The wolf leapt onto a rock and looked around attentively, his ears and tail outstretched, muzzle high. I started to climb the rock myself, but Mist jerked his head toward me and growled. If the wolf didn't want me to go up there with him, he must have had his reasons. So I stayed where I was and waited.

After a few moments, Mist lifted his head and let out a long howl. It was the first time I'd heard him howl since we'd set out together, and I watched in fascination. What exactly was he doing? Trying to communicate with someone? Who?

Suddenly, a shape emerged from the dark patch of the forest in front of us. Then another, and another, and another again. A wolf pack.

"Is that your pack, Mist?" I asked, full of amazement and relief. I was amazed because it meant that the wolves hadn't really disappeared, they'd simply hidden to escape the violence of humans. And I was relieved because Mist would be safe with his pack. They would protect each other, they wouldn't have let . . .

"Oh no," I muttered.

A huge black wolf, the first to emerge from the forest, was moving toward Mist with a menacing air. The rest of the pack stopped behind him and waited.

I didn't know anything about wolves. I had no idea how their relationships worked or how they communicated. But if they were anything like dogs . . . well, it was obvious that the black wolf was the leader of the pack and that he wasn't at all happy about Mist's return.

I studied the rest of the wolves behind him. All of them, male and female alike, had fur that was halfway between brown and red. Apart from four cubs, which were hopping around a female, whose coats were the same unmistakable color as Mist's. So that was his mate and those were his cubs. Perhaps Mist had been the leader of the pack when he was captured. Perhaps the black wolf was a usurper. What would happen now?

The wisest thing would have been to run away without waiting for an answer. I was in the middle of nowhere, miles and miles from the nearest town, and completely helpless in the face of a pack of wild creatures. Even though I had Brackenbury's rifles with me, the wolves would have killed me long before I could shoot one.

But . . . I couldn't run away. I couldn't leave without knowing what was going to happen to Mist. After everything we'd been through together, I wouldn't turn my back on him. I would stay with him until the end, whatever that might be.

Mist leapt down off the rock and moved toward the black wolf, stopping about ten yards from him. I looked around for somewhere safe and saw an old oak with low branches, I walked over to it and climbed up. Then, hugging the trunk of the tree, I watched the two animals getting ready to fight.

They both held their tails and heads high, as they stood motionless, studying each other. For a moment, time seemed to stop, and I fooled myself into thinking that nothing was going to happen.

But then the wolves bared their fangs, arched their backs, and attacked. Their violence reminded me of the violence of mud larks defending our territory. A violence without half measures. From the way Mist and the black wolf were fighting, I thought that probably only one of them would make it out alive. Just like with mud larks, only one gang gets control of the disputed territory.

For the first few minutes, neither wolf had the upper hand. But then the black wolf managed to bite Mist in the neck and throw him to the ground.

"No!" I screamed. "Come on, Mist! Fight!"

With a paw, Mist pushed the black wolf off him, and the two carried on fighting so ferociously I couldn't tell which one was winning. They made terrifying, angry noises, their fangs bared, and their gums glistening scarlet. I saw blood squirting and twice covered my eyes with my hands.

And then . . . Mist crushed the black wolf into the ground. He tried to get up, howling furiously, before collapsing onto his back, his stomach and throat exposed. Mist towered over him for about ten seconds, to make sure that his rival had really surrendered. Then he walked away, letting the other wolf get back on his feet. With his tail between his legs, the black wolf ran away and disappeared into the forest.

I couldn't believe my eyes. Mist had done it!

As soon as the black wolf was gone, Mist turned toward the tree where I'd taken refuge. I clambered down, almost falling because of the weight of the rifles. "I don't need them anymore," I muttered, throwing them away. Meanwhile, Mist had stopped a few yards off and was staring at me with his huge amber eyes.

"You did it, Mist," I said, looking at his pack waiting for him at the edge of the forest. "You're back home."

The wolf remained motionless, and I thought it was going to end like that. But I was wrong. Mist had a surprise for me. He came over, without taking his eyes off mine. Then he lowered his head and rubbed it against my belly. I stroked him instinctively, digging my fingers into the thick, shiny fur around his neck. It was the first time since the beginning of our friendship that the wolf had let me touch him. It was only a moment, unique and fleeting, but to me it was worth more than a thousand words or thank-yous.

"Good luck, Mist," I whispered.

The wolf took a few steps back and gave me a farewell look before returning to his pack. In an instant, they vanished into the forest, free and masters of their own destiny, as every animal deserves to be until the last day of its life.

As for me, I was ready to go back to the river, back to my family and my home.